THE
ONAWA
BESTIARY

by Henry D. M. Sherrerd, Jr.

The Onawa Bestiary

An opinionated survey with digressions

by
HENRY D. M. SHERRERD, Jr.

With drawings by
Douglas Bane

Additional drawings by William Massey III

The HarCroft Publishing Company
Hancock Point, Maine

Acknowledgements:
Page 60, from "Burnt Norton" in FOUR QUARTETS by T. S. Eliot, copyright 1943 by T. S. Eliot; renewed 1971 by Esme Valerie Eliot. Reprinted by permission of Harcourt Brace Jovanovich, Inc.
Pages 14-15, review of *Bumblebee Economics*, by Bernd Heinrich, written by Philip Morrison in Jan 1980 issue of *Scientific American*. Reprinted by permission of Philip Morrison.
Pages 17-18, "Flying Crooked," by Robert Graves, from *The Poems of Robert Graves*, Oxford University Press, New York, NY 1958. Reprinted by permission of the Publisher.
Design: Douglas R. Steinbauer

Library of Congress Cataloging-in-Publication Data
   Sherrerd, Henry D. M. 1928 -
     The Onawa Bestiary.
     Includes index.
     1. Zoology—Maine—Onawa Region. I. Title,
QL181.S54   1988   591.9741'25   87-17984
ISBN: 0-945432-01-1

Printed in the United States of America. Published by The HarCroft Publishing Company.

CONTENTS

To the memory of Ernest Thompson Seton

But ask now the beasts, and they shall
teach thee; and the fowls of the air, and they
shall tell thee:

Or speak to the earth, and it shall teach
thee; and the fishes of the sea shall declare
unto thee.

— Job XII

List of Illustrations

FOREWORD   ✳ I first became acquainted with Henry Sherrerd's writing a couple of years ago. Susan Abel, the eminently capable librarian at the Abbott Memorial Library in Dexter, showed me something called *The Onawa Bestiary*. She said she thought that I would like it. Since she's usually right about such matters, I took the book home and read it. She was right again.

The "Bestiary" that I saw then was one of a few that Sherrerd had had printed and bound as gifts for friends. It immediately became apparent to me that the work demanded a far wider audience, and I am delighted to be a part of giving it just that.

I read somewhere that a good writer possesses qualities of 'close observation and independently arrived-at conclusions.' I feel that Sherrerd's work meets these criteria very well. Consider his remarks upon the muskrat: "Their naked, rat-like tails are flattened in the vertical plane; ... but the visual effect is more like that of being closely followed by a snake." Or, "Nuthatches are nutty birds not only because they insist on coming down a tree headfirst, unlike any sensible bird; they are also the world's most picky birds." Or bumblebees: "I am aware that my feelings have always been friendly, in marked contrast to the case for other bees, wasps, and hornets. It may have something to do with the size and rotundity of the insect; fatness is somehow comical (why are pigs and hippos inherently comical?) and doubly so when banded with yellow-orange and black."

A glance at Sherrerd's autobiographical sketch (pp 148) reveals that his formal education firmly grounded him in the classics, and this is confirmed in his text. From the Bible to Dante to Darwin—Athena to Rabelais to Eliot—classical allusions abound. These references serve to enrich his descriptions of animal life, life that might seem prosaic to others but never to Sherrerd.

The author of *The Onawa Bestiary* is that anomaly, the writer with the mind of a scientist but the soul of a poet. Here he is on a flock of sandpipers: "Smokelike, diaphanous, endlessly changing its form from a compact mass to a wavering filament: a living arabesque modulating to a secret rhythm—". Spider webs: "... delicate works of art strung with dew-pearls on a foggy morning— ... Until the advent of nylon monofilament it was one of the strongest materials known for its weight ..." On the movement of water striders: "One can almost see the grid of cartesian coordinates as the strider moves from $X2Y3$ to $X5Y7$ ...;" but he's human, too: "... there is something immensely satisfying about dropping a stone in the middle of a patch of striders."

So, we have the observations of a "nature lover," a scientist, a poet—yes, and of a humorist, because for all his technical background, Henry has a wry, self-deprecating sense of fun that manifests itself throughout the pages. It is the amusement that is to be found when a person doesn't mind having animals play tricks upon him, or when he sees sheldrakes as Keystone Kops, or a loitering sunfish as the tough kid on the block.

It is my pleasure and honor to be a small part of Henry Sherrerd's first published book. I say "first" because it is apparent that there must be others to follow.

Gerald E. Lewis
Garland, Maine
April 12, 1986

INTRODUCTION   ∗ The short definition of a bestiary is that it is "a moralizing treatise on animals." A fuller explanation is that it is "a work which describes the alleged habits of various beasts [hence the name] following each account by an interpretation giving its moral or theological significance." T. H. White, in his translation of a 12th-century Latin bestiary, calls it "a serious work of natural history." This book offers a good deal of moralizing and interpretation (not necessarily serious) but very little theology. Instead, the scope is expanded as indicated by the subtitle, and to understand better many of the digressions the reader should know something of the background and history of the Onawa area.

The most important fact about Onawa is that it is very isolated on the eastern edge of the Longfellow Mountains in central Maine, in Elliotsville Plantation Township of Piscataquis County. It lies in the wilderness southeast of Greenville, northeast of Monson, northwest of Dover-Foxcroft, and southwest of Mt. Katahdin. Onawa is in the middle of nowhere, and would surely have remained just another inaccessible mountain lake had not the trans-Maine course of the Canadian Pacific Railroad taken it near the south shore in

1889. The CPRR begat the village of Onawa; a station, water tower, general store, and ten or a dozen railroad workers' homes. In turn, the village begat a small summer colony of about 20 camps along the south shore and another 16 uplake on sheltered coves and islands. For transportation, communication, and supplies, village and camps alike were dependent on the Scoot, the local train from Brownville Junction to Greenville and back every day. The only other access was by a tortuous logging road around Borestone Mountain to the Bodfish Valley, and a mile of woods-trail ending on Long Pond Stream.

Nevertheless, Onawa remained isolated and static. The paper company that owned most of the Plantation at the turn of the century would sell no more land, nor would any of the various succeeding companies, so once the initial period of settlement was over no further expansion was possible. No roads were built; no more camps; no hotels or clubs; no tourist trade nor any other kind of shops, restaurants, theatres, markets, nor businesses of any kind; nothing. Onawa was frozen in time for the better part of 50 years, and neither grew nor prospered.

Such thaw as did occur came very slowly. Ice boxes were replaced by propane-burning refrigerators only in the late 40s; telephone lines reached the lake in the late 50s; a graveled road to the south shore was constructed in the 60s to maintain some sort of access after the Scoot was discontinued and the village rapidly withered away; electricity followed the road in 1977, and along the south shore at least the original Spartan (even Puritanical) back-to-nature way of life far from the maddening crowd and unhealthy vapors—the summer heat—of the big cities finally gave way in the 80s to whatever is meant by the term "lifestyle." The uplake camps, on the other hand, still live more or less in the Edwardian Age, dependent on boats for transportation and kerosene lamps for light. At times Onawa may sound like a small, exclusive, posh resort—a sort of unknown Lake Placid—but it is not. It is still much as it was nearly a hundred years ago: a collection of summer camps in the wilderness, most of them handed down through three and even four generations. Which is why the wildlife is still around to be observed, enjoyed, and in some cases eaten.

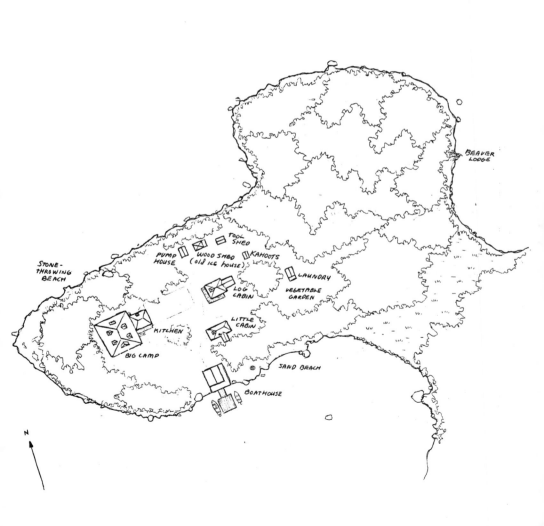

BEAVER
LODGE

STONE-
THROWING
BEACH

TOOL
SHED

PUMP
HOUSE

WOOD SHED
(old ice house)

KAHOOTS

LAUNDRY

LOG
CABIN

VEGETABLE
GARDEN

KITCHEN

LITTLE
CABIN

BIG CAMP

SAND BEACH

BOATHOUSE

N

✳ When the old boathouse burned in 1971 it was bad
enough to lose all those boats, motors, tools, stored
furniture and kitchenware, lumber and repair supplies,
the accumulated odds and ends of 80 years—and I
don't even want to think about the totem poles and
three generations worth of family memories—it was
bad enough, I say, to lose all that; but one of the
greatest losses may well have been the bat colony that
lived in the front roof dormer. This was a small,
triangular blind dormer set low on the porch roof facing
the ramp and dock. In keeping with the totem-poles
supporting the porch roof and other carvings, it was
richly ornamented. Split cedar logs carved with lightning bolts, painted bright yellow against dark blue,
were nailed to the sides. At the base of the triangle was
an 8-inch plank carved with the camp motto:

CHAÇUN À SON GÔUT

which pleased my father—and doubtless the ghost of
Rabelais—but was thought to be hardly the case. Particularly in the old days of carefully planned activities,
formal visits to Aunt Minnie, no card games on Sunday,
and a (supposedly) total ban on any alcohol other than
the kitchen supply of vanilla extract. Within the triangle was an ancient sailing-canoe sideboard carved with
three stylized pine trees representative of the rather
unoriginal camp name, "The Pines." Neither Grandmother (a true grande-dame of the old school) nor anyone else much liked the name, but we were stuck with
it since Dr. Sanden, who built the camp in 1892, had
had all the flatware so stamped.

In the midst of this more-than-oriental-splendor lived a major bat colony. In daytime the bats were dormant, and many a person who walked or stood and talked beneath the dormer would have panicked had they known what was immediately overhead. Only in the late afternoon did the colony begin to make itself known. There would be secretive rustlings, little scrabbling noises, occasional very high-pitched squeals and chittering. The bats were getting up. As the light faded this activity increased accordingly, and it was impossible not to feel that the bats were getting themselves organized and deciding what to do and where to go. At sundown they launched, and that is more than a mere figure of speech. One by one they appeared in a crack at the lower end of the right-hand lightning bolt, hesitated a moment, then launched themselves much like a carrier catapulting its fighters. For ten minutes or more they poured out, regular as clockwork. I never timed the interval, regrettably enough, but one every six seconds seems about right and that would make a total of some 100, which is also about right. It seemed like a lot more, and no one disputed Chet Drew's observation that "they must be a million of 'em in there . . ."

There are still plenty of bats around—in the evening there are likely to be a dozen or more flittering about over the cove, the lawn, the old croquet court, and everywhere else. I like to watch them as they go through the same marvelously intricate, though less graceful, aerobatics as the swallows. But mostly I like to think about the vast quantities of mosquitoes, minges, black flies, no-see-ums and other miseries that they consume. In *Wild Animals of North America* (National Geographic Society, 1979) it is stated that a colony of 500 little brown bats (which is what we have at Onawa) will eat 500,000 insects in a night. If the old boathouse colony was truly 100 strong, that is 100,000 insects, and if it was only 50 that is still 50,000 plagues less per night. Hence my lament for the loss. And while such matters are difficult if not impossible to quantify, I do feel that mosquitoes were less of a problem in those days. Even if the figures are off by a factor of 10 or more, that is still a lot of itching that never happened, and the occasional clean-up job necessary when one or two bats find their way in to roost in a cabin is a small price indeed to pay for such an efficient service.

* During those years when bear hunting was unrestricted, Onawa suffered an annual invasion of what can only be described as a task force of redneck good ol' boys. They would arrive in three or four pickup trucks filled with cages of tracking hounds; large, beefy, unshaven, sweaty men wearing dirty T-shirts, armed with huge rifles, western-style single-action revolvers, hunting knives the size of the Roman short sword, and many cases of beer. If there was no wind the distant baying of the hounds and occasional shots could be heard all day. Even the most dedicated of the local hunters disapproved of the whole affair.

On one such day I was working around the boathouse, listening to the dogs and estimating their progress as they moved slowly north along the lower slopes of Borestone Mountain, directly across the lake. There were no shots, so I had hopes for the bear. Ayako (my Japanese wife) had gone fishing not long before, and thus I was surprised when her boat came skimming around the point and made a sort of controlled crash-landing at the dock. She was halfway between hysteria and hilarity as she told her story:

She had anchored at the inlet where a slight breeze positioned the boat to face northeast. There was nothing to do but admire the view, throw back the occasional chub, and watch a nearby loon. The loon dived and did not reappear—where was it coming up this time? She turned to face southwest and saw a large, dark *something* swimming toward her, no more than a boatlength away. A big dog? Oh no—a bear! She screamed; she beat the water with her fishing rod; she pulled the starter-rope on the motor. The motor caught at once, the boat lurched away dragging both fishline and anchor, and the bear abandoned any ideas of climbing aboard and turned toward Birch Island, 100 yards away. Safely out of range, Ayako watched it swim on, clamber over the shoreline rocks, shake itself like a great shaggy mop, and disappear into the trees. It was, she said, the biggest bear she had ever seen outside a zoo. Nothing monstrous, but a *big* bear.

And a smart one. At about the time all this happened I estimated the hunters, or at least the dogs, were still no further north along Borestone than Cumming's Point, which is a good half mile from the Inlet Point where the bear must have started swimming.

If that was a very smart and wary bear, another one we encountered was surely one of the most stupid and careless. We were walking the Barren logging road, partridge hunting in October. The day was calm, clear, and warm. Many leaves had fallen, but many were still on the trees; it was gorgeous as we wandered along. Partridge being what they are, we were not talking and were moving as quietly as possible. Where the road was covered with leaves this was difficult, but other stretches were bare sand and gravel and we moved in silence. So it was that we heard something rustling the leaves off to the side up ahead. We stopped and listened: partridge? red squirrel? deer? We moved on slowly, and shortly came to a break in the roadside screen of shrubs that opened onto a thinly-wooded uphill slope. Twenty yards away was a small bear, pawing and snuffling among the dead leaves, most probably looking for beechnuts.

Because experience has taught us that a shotgun is almost useless for deep-woods partridge hunting, we both carry .22 rifles and stalk the bird after its initial flight. On this occasion Ayako had her Browning .22 automatic, but I was carrying a scoped Winchester .22 Hornet varmint rifle—deadly accurate out to 175 yards—for the possible long-range shot far up the road. This is by no means a big-game rifle, but it is quite capable of taking deer and similar-sized animals with a well-placed shot. For this bear, and at close range, it would have been more than adequate.

I raised the rifle and sighted on the back of its head.

The bear continued to poke around in the leaves, noisy as ever. I sighted on the shoulder. I sat down for a steadier hold and sighted on the ear, then the back of the head again as it turned slightly. I let the safety off and began to tighten on the trigger, thought that all unknowingly the bear was a thirty-second of an inch and a tightened muscle away from death, put the safety back on and stood up. The bear went on shuffling leaves. We watched for another few minutes as it wandered slowly up-slope, then walked on. It would have been too much like shooting someone raiding the icebox before going to bed for the long, cold winter.

Finally, there is Bettison's Bear, which we had less to do with yet knew more intimately than any other. In the fall of 1976 Sherwood Copeland shot a fine fat bear in prime condition, not far from the CPRR tracks on the side of Benson Mountain. A nearby repair crew let him borrow their motorized handcar, so he ran the bear back to Onawa and dressed it out properly. The skin was sent off to be tanned and made into a rug for Lindley Bettison: it had been a standing order for some years should the opportunity arise. The meat was distributed among the few people still at Onawa, and thus Ayako and I happened to receive a couple of goodlooking steaks. We were both dubious about such meat, Ayako mainly on the grounds of total unfamiliarity, and I because I had heard so many stories about bear meat being tough, gamy, and smelly. But this looked good, and since I am willing to try anything once Ayako broiled it for me for dinner. She refused to touch it until my comments on how good it was, much to my surprise, goaded her into a taste—then another, and another, and shortly it was all gone. Perfectly delicious; as good meat as either of us ever ate. So now, whenever there is a party at Bettison's and someone admires the thick, heavy bearskin rug before the hearth, we have the ultimate in one-upsmanship comments: "You don't know the half of it—he was even better to eat."

D. Bane

* Red squirrels may be a nuisance around camp, but beavers are a positive menace. Where the red squirrel will make a mess of things should it get into a cabin, a beaver can destroy a small cabin by felling a tree across it. This has not happened at my camp or any other that I know of, admittedly, but the potential is there. Marvelous engineers that they are, a felled tree doesn't always go just where they want it; one does not need to walk far along a wooded shoreline to find such hung-up evidence.

And it is no good saying they fell only poplar trees. Quite the contrary. Around Onawa the only tree that seems immune to beaver-attack is the pine, and even that is not safe if the beaver is hungry enough—or has no sense of taste. I have never seen a felled pine, but I have seen a few that were partially chewed. Not by porcupines, either; beaver tooth marks are unmistakable. So it was that in the fall of 1967 we had to wire-wrap all the poplars around camp after the beavers built a lodge out on the back cove and cut half a dozen big poplars before we realized what was happening. The screen and chicken-wire scraps are still in place, now tight as a drum where the trees have grown into the originally-loose wrapping. This was an effective counter measure; there was no more local cutting

BEAVERS

around my point, and a year later the lodge was abandoned.

In the fall of 1979, however, the beavers re-occupied the lodge—although I had always been told they would not return to an old lodge—and began decimating the maple and birch around the camp complex, not far out on the back point as before. Aside from their ornamental and wind-screening value, this was a real and present danger in the case of some of the big birches near the cabins. In the midst of all the other closing-up preparations, then, we had to raid the old dump for some more rusty chicken wire and spend a day wrapping every birch and maple that seemed worth saving or that might fall across a cabin.

Another fallacy concerning beavers is that they are silent; voiceless, even. They certainly work silently—except when the tree falls—and swim as quietly as a muskrat—except for the tail-slapping alarm signal that if you are unprepared can make you wonder who fired that .45—but voiceless? No. At least not when in the throes of passion. Ayako and I were once trolling along the Barren shore in the late afternoon when we saw two beavers swimming nose-to-tail some distance ahead. Slowly we overtook them, and as they neither dove nor altered course in the least, I pulled off to the side and paralleled them at 10 yards or so. Oblivious to the boat, they continued swimming, and since the 5½ HP motor is very quiet at trolling speed we could hear one of them making a strange sort of strangled noise halfway between a grunt and a squeal. If it is possible for a wild animal to make an indecent noise, that was it. Whether it came from the male or female was impossible to tell. Assuming they *were* male and female; that was also impossible to tell—and at the same time impossible to think anything else.

Watching the beavers as we slowly pulled ahead we saw them begin swimming in a wide circle, and then they were lost to us around a point. We trolled on for 10 or 15 minutes, turned, and headed back along the same track. As we came around the point in the now-failing light we saw the beavers still in the same area, still swimming nose-to-tail about a foot apart, and as we passed them still making that noise. Feeling somewhat as though we had just heard, but not seen, an X-rated nature film, we left them in peace.

BLACK FLIES

* @-=**%&@$!+)*~?!&//'[]*%-! little bastards! I know they have a place in the overall scheme of things; I have gutted too many trout and salmon and found them packed solid with black flies not to appreciate their usefulness in the ecological food chain. But I still say @-=++'~%-@$&(*^))%-!!!

There is also this thought: ". . . behold, I will send swarms of flies upon thee, and upon thy servants, and upon thy people, and into thy houses; and the houses of the Egyptians shall be full of swarms of flies, and also the ground whereon they are."

When the Lord threatened Pharoah with this most maddening of all plagues, He was talking about common, everyday, garden-variety houseflies, right? Wrong. Anyone who has spent time in the Maine woods in June knows He meant black flies. Houseflies are disgusting in swarming around garbage and dead meat; black flies are irresistibly drawn to warm, walking-around, live people. The Lord is more subtle and terrifying in power than you think.

BLUEJAYS ✱ Bluejays are raucous, aggressive birds whose only saving grace may be their colorfulness. Other small birds obviously fear them. At feeding time on the kitchen porch the usual collection of sparrows, chickadees, nuthatches, and juncos will pay no attention to most of the larger birds that may join them or happen to be nearby, but they will scatter instantly at the appearance of a bluejay. Although I have never seen a bluejay attack a smaller bird, they are generally credited with doing so, and more particularly with eating both eggs and nestlings. Or maybe it is the bluejay's constant scolding that is so annoying; who wants to eat dinner with a gaudily overdressed, overbearing screamer?

On the other hand, all that noise leads to interesting speculation. Bluejays are considered the very bane of hunters; they are natural alarm signals, warning deer, squirrels, and any other game of potential danger. So when I hear bluejays yelling far off in the woods— and if one is loud, a whole flock of them can be heard for a long way on a quiet day—I wonder what's going on? At times I have used this uproar in reverse, letting the bluejay be my guide instead of announcer. While I keep hoping it will be a covey of partridge or something interesting like a bobcat, it is usually a red squirrel, raven, owl, or other animal that bluejays don't get along with. For that matter, bluejays don't seem to get along with anything except other bluejays, although they occasionally try through mimicry. I have watched a bluejay successively reproduce the song of the car-

dinal, robin, tufted titmouse, and several other familiar
songbirds. What is the point of it, I wonder? The purpose of visual mimicry is obvious: to escape being
eaten by looking like a twig, leaf, or something known
to taste bad, or as camouflage when approaching
prey—but audio mimicry? To attract a potential dinner? Yet bluejays are not *that* predatory.

So bluejays are not particularly attractive birds.
But it could be worse. At least they don't make a career
of stealing things as their first cousin the Canada Jay
does. The Whiskey Jack or Camp Robber is aptly
named; in the Yukon I have had one filch a ¼-pound
arctic greyling from a rock immediately behind me
while I fished for more. Brook trout caught along the
streams that run into Onawa are too hard to come by to
even consider that sort of thing.

BOBCATS * They're around, but I have never seen one and probably never will unless I am very fortunate. For that matter, not many of the old-timers and natives have seen them either. In a lifetime spent in the woods around Onawa, Sherwood Copeland says he has shot two bobcats and seen no more than perhaps three or four others. Elmer Berg remembers hearing bobcats in a few occasions, but only once actually meeting one; it was watching him from the top of the rock-cut by the old CPRR water tank. So Bruce Andrews, who spent only three years at the store, was very fortunate to catch something more than a fleeting glimpse of a bobcat. It was in action. On a calm, quiet day in mid-winter as Bruce was shoveling snow from the roof of the Herbert camp at Sand Beach, he heard Budweiser, his beagle, break into voice off in the woods to the west. Bud had found a rabbit, of course, but where was he? Bruce climbed back to the ridge, looked around—and out into the snowcovered ice of the cove ran a bobcat, with Bud in hot pursuit. Fascinated, Bruce watched the chase proceed until he suddenly realized the potential danger. The snow crust was not that strong; should the bobcat decide to turn and fight, Bud would have no chance as soon as he broke through with his short legs and small feet. So Bruce yelled. Loudly. More startled than ever, the bobcat ran off even faster and Bud reluctantly abandoned the chase, never understanding how close he may have been to the fight of, and for, his life.

I'd like to have seen that, but I am limited to fresh tracks in the snow, the remains of a kill (see *deer*, page

D. Banej

31) and finding what was probably a bobcat den in a split boulder in Flood Cove. For an animal that is common if not plentiful, the bobcat has a remarkable ability to stay out of sight. It is not that the bobcat is shy in the sense that deer are shy, say—quite the contrary. To use that word in describing a bobcat is about like saying a barracuda is shy. Fighting like a wildcat, after all, is the standard phrase for all-out fury. No; bobcats are simply solitary in the extreme, taking far more care than any other animals to remain unseen. Perhaps it is just as well.

BUMBLEBEES   ✱ Certainly one of the most charming of all Emerson's poems is *The Humble-Bee*, with such memorable lines as "Thou animated torrid-zone!" and "Sailor of the atmosphere; / Swimmer through the waves of air;". In addition to the sweet, gentle tone the poem is also a careful observation of the bumblebee's habits. Either by direct statement or inference the bumblebee is characterized as living in the four-seasons New England climate, more solitary than the well-organized honeybee, gathering from a variety of wildflowers (thirteen are named) and hibernating for the winter. Emerson wrote a lovely poem and got his facts straight as well—a rather unusual occurrence in poetry.

Bumblebees seem to affect people that way. For example: Philip Morrison's book review of *Bumblebee Economics*, by Bernd Heinrich, in the January 1980 issue of *Scientific American*. Morrison is a fine lecturer and writer as well as a physicist, more in the manner of Bronowski than Sagan. His reviews are always thoughtful and perceptive, but this one is unique for its combination of factual information and graceful phrasing. He begins:

> It might be anywhere in the temperate U.S. where morning sunlight falls on some moist meadow. A shadowed woodland is not far off, and nearby too may be a quiet pond, where beavers silently glide. In the spring a flycatcher calls; later on stands of high-bush blueberry and jewelweed come to decorate the spot. Insistent little furry,

aerial forms in orange and black dart among the blossoms. The simple sense of leisure is our own sunny reverie; here we are watching the work of a hard-pressed economy. Bumblebees (there are 50 species over the U.S. and Canada . . .) have been inlaid within the complex of tundra life for tens of millions of years by the deftest of invisible hands. Found now in all kinds of open areas—fields, roadside, and mountaintop—bumblebees are best adapted to the flora of the slowly changing bogs that mark the cool woodland, relics of the ancient tundra.

And ends:

> . . . There is a Maine ambience in this displaced New Englander's writing: every chapter bears an epigraph, often one from a New England poet. The book itself is a concentrate of goodness. Not least is the indirect light it casts on human beings, that single species so swift to change and so varied in social structure that its diverse patterns of behavior worldwide can hardly be the work of the same invisible slow forces that have exquisitely sorted the genes of the bumblebee throughout the Cenozoic.

Like Emerson, Heinrich and Morrison have been captivated by the bumblebee—and I am right there with them, wondering just why this should be so. I have never spent a great deal of time thinking about bumblebees, but I am aware that my feelings have always been friendly, in marked contrast to the case for the other bees, wasps, and hornets. It may have something to do with the size and rotundity of the insect; fatness is somehow comical (why are pigs and hippos inherently comical?) and doubly so when banded with yellow-orange and black. The bumbling aspect is also involved. The honeybee is all too businesslike, and much too quick to sting when disturbed, but the bumblebee does seem to go blundering along from flower to flower in a much more haphazard, what-the-hell manner—and I know of no one ever stung by a bumblebee. I frequently find bumblebees in the boathouse, buzzing vainly against the windows, then backing off and charging at full speed as if remembering the old adage, "when all else fails, use brute force." They hit the glass with a sharp crack like flicking a finger against a window, and about as forceful. Honeybees never get in the boathouse to begin with, and wasps are summarily dispatched, but bumblebees are gently chased out.

There is also the bumblebee's singleness, or aloneness, in contrast to the swarming behavior of most insects, which imparts a certain air of individuality and character. The only time I can recall seeing more than two or three bumblebees in the same area was one summer when a patch of very low, thickly-matted weed in the grass beside the boathouse path suddenly bloomed with tiny skyblue flowers. For a week you could hardly see the flowers for the bumblebees that covered the whole patch. Whether this flowering weed was a favorite that had never bloomed before, or an opportunistic find is debatable, but the message got around quickly, and it seemed as if every bumblebee in the Onawa basin was there. On looking it up, the weed turned out to be named self-heal or all-heal; an herb, in fact. I am still trying to determine what relationship it has to Emerson's "Succory to match the sky." Succory is the old name for chicory, which is a much taller, daisy-like plant—but aside from the blue flower in both cases there might be something similar in the pollen that drives the bumblebees out of their furry little gourds.

D. Bane

BUTTERFLIES

* The butterflies common around Onawa are in no way remarkable as far as I know, but then I know nothing about butterflies. There are Monarchs, Tiger Swallow-tails, a medium-sized blackwinged species, and many pale off-white sorts. I enjoy watching them all and can think of nothing to say about them that is not already perfectly summed up in a poem by Robert Graves:

Flying Crooked*

The butterfly, a Cabbage White,
(His honest idiocy of flight)
Will never now, it is too late,
Master the art of flying straight,

The Poems of Robert Graves, Doubleday Anchor Books, Doubleday & Co., Inc. Garden City, NY 1958.

Yet has—who knows so well as I?—
A just sense of how not to fly:
He lurches here and here by guess
And God and hope and hopelessness.
Even the aerobatic swift
Has not his flying-crooked gift.

Graves is actually talking about a lot more here than mere butterflies, and since it could apply to my own life just as well as his, I will say no more.

* Canadian Geese do not live at Onawa, but they will **CANADIAN** occasionally spend the night in the course of their **GEESE** migrations. They never land until the last light, sometimes coming into the inlet swamp, sometimes into Duck Cove, and sometimes they will settle down along the gravel bar north of our point. On a calm evening their gabbling carries across the water clearly but indistinctly, and the effect is that of listening to a big party across the lake—except that it is long past the party season.

When they do not stop but pass in great "V"'s overhead—well, if you have not seen, and heard, and been profoundly moved by this, then you have no idea what life in the north woods is all about. So I will tell you:

Metamorphosis

For Sam

I like to think that I am
Pretty civilized, and I could
Hardly help it after all those

Years and years of Education,
And training in the niceties of
Holding coats and doors and chairs,
Walking on the curbstone side,
And mouthing the polite response
Among the social silverware.
And I have even earned my bread
In war and peace as requisite
By intellect alone, so that
If what remains of animal in me
Were sloughed away, presumably
There should be something left.
But all that vanishes like
Bright fantastic visions at the
Snap of the enchanter's fingers
When I hear the high clear
Laughing call of wavering
Echelons of northbound geese.

✻ There aren't any now and haven't been since 1898, **CARIBOU**
when (reputedly) the last few in the area were seen
heading out of Monson toward Borestone Mountain. On
Borestone itself the ancient migration trail survives as
one of the pathways near Terris Moore's camp on Sunset Pond.✻ The path leads around the edge of the pond
and is not frequently traveled—hardly at all, in fact. Yet
it is a distinct channel through the forest floor, in places
as much as six inches or more below the general level.
There never were and never will be enough people on
Borestone to make a trail like that, and although deer
and moose have something to do with it their movement is far too random to account fully for such wear.
But caribou migrate with great regularity, and this trail
is the evidence of many, many animals and thousands
of years.

There are other reminders of caribou in the area.

---

*Turned over to The National Audubon Society in 1985. The
ponds, camp and top of the mountain now form the Borestone
Mountain Sanctuary.

Just east of Onawa on the other side of Benson Mountain in T7R9† is a large swamp called Caribou Bog, even on the U. S. Geodetic Survey map. In the golden era (the teens and twenties) of Noisy Brook Camp on Benson Pond some two miles to the southwest, it was a favorite deer hunting territory. But great-grandfather Henry D. Moore hunted the region long before that—he first came to it in the early 1890s with an old friend from the 2nd Maine Cavalry of Civil War times—and the chances are good that he saw some of the last caribou. Probably shot at them as well. Unfortunately he did not begin keeping his hunting diary until 1907, and while everything else is carefully chronicled, there is no mention of caribou either at the time or "in the old days." A pity: it would be wonderful to be able to prove that caribou were still around that late.

Descriptions of caribou always point out how well-insulated the animal is (which ought to be obvious considering where it lives) due to the heavy coat complete with hollow guard-hairs. This is one of those gee-whiz facts I can confirm. Terris has a has a caribou skin issued to him by the Canadian IGY Scientific Party as a routine item of arctic survival gear when, in 1958, he was flying for them around Ellesmere Island in his very special Piper Cub. The skin is big enough to lie on comfortably, about two inches thick, dense as felt, and resilient as a sponge. Terris claims nothing else is needed between you and the ice, and I believe it. I have never seen an animal skin anything like it.

---

†Township 7, Range 9: unorganized and unnamed.

CARPENTER ANTS

* To be industrious as an ant is the equivalent of being busy as a beaver, but while I approve the principle I deplore the practice in this case. Beavers are constructive; even if they cut a lot of trees in the process they produce something real, solid, and certainly long-lasting in their lodges and dams. And something of great benefit to the rich and varied wildlife living in and around the ponds so created. Why can't carpenter ants be similarly industrious about something besides destroying the foundation posts and framework of "The Pines," which benefits nobody?

Replacing foundation-posts once in a while is no big deal, but finding that a whole wall is a mere shell because the carpenter ants have honeycombed the two-by-four interior structure is upsetting in the extreme. So when the ants swarm out of their underground nests along the hard-packed earth on and near the boathouse path, winged for the appropriate time and occasion, I am after them with a spray-can of flying-insect killer and a vindictiveness that rarely surfaces in my uncommonly sweet and gentle nature.

Carpenter ants indeed! Never was a creature so misnamed; carpenters build things—they don't destroy them. I prefer the term used by the family gardener/handyman long ago in South Jersey. His terminology was inaccurate and he was referring to a different species of insect, but he sure as hell had the right idea. He called them "turmoils."

CHICKADEES ✱ To the chickadees in 1975 I was a moveable feast. That was the year I hand-tamed a small flock that lived around camp, and so had to carry a pocketful of sunflower seeds wherever I went. At the boathouse, the pumphouse, the tool shed, sitting in a boat working on a motor, clearing alders in the old garden, picking up driftwood on the stone-throwing beach—no matter where, I would hear that familiar "dee-dee-dee" and look around to see who wanted to be fed. Or look up to find the bird hovering in front of my face. It was delightful; never have I had such a companionable summer.

Chickadees are everyone's favorite, like chipmunks and for very much the same reason. Small, bright-eyed, neatly-colored, active and acrobatic—they spend more time upside-down than any other bird except the nuthatch—there is a basic attractiveness about them that is heightened by their obvious interest in man and his affairs. I have many times been trailed through the woods by chickadees, and if I sit quietly they will flit around the nearest twigs and branches with apparent curiosity. I remember with particular pleasure the day I went bear hunting with Sam Aertker. We separated towards the end of our slow climb up Barren Mountain, and thus I arrived at the base of the rockfall alone. I found one of those lovely spots where a huge moss-covered boulder at once commands a magnificent view, yet is sheltered within a spruce thicket. Sitting there in the early-morning sun, watching the lingering patches of fog disperse in the coves far below—we had started well before dawn—it was one of those golden moments that was improved no end by the half-dozen chickadees that joined me. Not in the least afraid, they would, I felt quite sure, have come to my hand had I anything to offer other than a chocolate bar. Since I really didn't care that much about shooting a bear, it was by far the best part of the hunt.

* If it weren't for the fact that its tail is thinly-furred **CHIPMUNKS**
under the best of conditions and downright scraggly
most of the time, the chipmunk could serve as the
original model for the phrase "bright-eyed and bushy-
tailed." As there is something inherently comical about
frogs, so there is a basic attractiveness about the chipmunk that makes it everybody's favorite wild animal—
although it is so easily tamed it is hard to think of a
chipmunk as wild. Every camp around the lake has its
family of tame chipmunks that will beg for sunflower
seeds even at the height of the most raucous party.
Indeed, they are so much a part of daily life, like a pet
dog or cat, that it is surprising to encounter one out in
the woods that merely watches instead of running up
for a handout.

Chipmunks are usually called "Chips" or
"Chippy" except at our camp; there the term is
"Stripes" no matter which of those in residence is
being addressed. There is always one that can be iden-
tified by battle-scars—missing patches of fur, occasional bloodstains—that is presumably the dominant
male. This one we refer to as "Old Stripes," and I often
wonder how old he really is. Certainly he lives several
years, becomes very tame, and has a memory that
spans at least six months. When opening camp in the
spring we are frequently met on the kitchen porch by

such a chipmunk. We trudge up the path from the boathouse laden like packhorses with gear and supplies; if Old Stripes is not waiting at the top of the steps he is sure to appear before the load is dumped and the door-shutter removed. This is not an invariable routine, but it happens often enough to assure us that it is the same Old Stripes we left in charge of the camp at the end of October—if he was still awake.

Although chipmunks hibernate, their schedule seems pretty flexible. We expect to lose them toward the end of October when the fall rains set in, but sometimes they will disappear in the midst of beautiful weather in September—and then reappear a few weeks later on a cold, gray, rainy day one would think the clearest of all possible signals that it is time for the long winter sleep. They don't stay around long on such occasions, but it is odd. Particularly when they don't seem to be affected by a real Indian Summer that ought to bring them popping out of their holes and bounding around the place as if they were on springs. The biological clock, it would appear, is not that carefully regulated.

Or it may be that a chipmunk's clock is designed for longterm effects, in that hibernation offsets speeded-up daily activity. Surely a chipmunk lives in another dimension of time where things happen much faster. A chipmunk moves so quickly that it really cannot be seen in the act of moving, but rather in the split-second intervals between movements. It is like looking at one of the old thumb-flip picture books. Only when sweeping up the birdseed on the kitchen porch does a chipmunk appear to move in anything close to normal time, but even then its tail flicks from up to down position much too fast to be seen. After six months of such fast living it is no wonder a chipmunk needs six months of sleep.

Then again, hibernation may be a myth, and chipmunks actually spend all winter living a normal routine underground while gorging on the prodigious amounts of food stored away. I have never kept track of the total amount of sunflower and birdseed bought during any given season, but it runs to a good many pounds and the birds get only a small portion of it. I generally throw out a couple of handfuls before every meal so we can watch the small birds and chipmunks as we eat. A chipmunk working its way through scattered seed is just the reverse of a boat on calm water; it leaves a perfectly clean wake. With cheek-pouches distended to the bursting point, its head is held noticeably lower as it scampers off to unload. One of the silliest things I ever saw occurred at such a time. The chipmunk looked as if it had a ping-pong ball in each cheek as it ran off the porch and followed its usual trail which led back under the porch. At that time the supporting structure of the porch was screened by upright logs about six inches in diameter, closely fitted for the most part but necessarily with many gaps more than wide enough for a chipmunk to slip through under normal circumstances. So whether this chipmunk forgot how much it had increased its own width, or was trying a narrower, unfamiliar gap is a moot question, but it bounced back its own length and more when it hit the gap at full speed. It would be fun to report that the whole cheeks-load was jettisoned forth in true animated-cartoon fashion, but this did not happen; the chipmunk merely picked itself up and found a wider gap.

One final note on a chipmunk's cheek-pouch capacity: from time to time we have fed them counted numbers of sunflower seeds to see how many they can hold. The average is about 50 to 55, but there was one who packed in 80 seeds! The last few kept dribbling out and had to be jammed back in several times. It was like nothing so much as Red Skelton's famous routine of the bum at the free-lunch counter. Nature imitating art? Whatever, it was hysterical.

CORMORANTS ✻ Along the Maine coast a cormorant is called a "shag," but at Onawa they aren't called much of anything except maybe "those funny-looking ducks (or gulls)." Most people don't know what they are, of course, because Onawa people are lake-dwellers. Being true woods hermits, the natives never go anywhere at all if possible, and certainly no farther than Monson, Guilford, Dover-Foxcroft, or Greenville when absolutely necessary. The summer people have a nodding acquaintance with the South Jersey shore, but the beach at Ocean City and such resorts offers little to look at besides sandpipers, herring gulls, and far too many people. No one would mistake a pelican or penguin, say, if either should appear at Onawa (*die mirabilis!*) as such birds are too often seen on TV or in the *National Geographic* to be missed—but cormorants are erratic visitors to Onawa and are basically unknown.

They never stay long when they do appear, and it is just as well they don't hang around. The fishing is bad enough in Onawa, and, considering the amount of fingerling and bigger trout and salmon that must be taken by the normal population of loons and Sheldrake, the last thing in the world Onawa needs is a flock of birds with the fish-eating reputation of the cormorant. Still, I like the thought of catching a bunch of them, tying cords around those snake-like necks and letting them fish for me in proper oriental fashion—at night, with a pine-knot torch burning on a bracket out over the bow of the boat. And I like to see one occasionally sitting on the big rock 50 yards or so off the dock, with wings spread to dry and looking like nothing so much as a living Teutonic coat of arms.

* There are few sounds as soothing and relaxing as **CRICKETS**
the cricket song, and it is no wonder the cricket-on-the-
hearth is the universal symbol of domestic tranquillity.
Occidentals think of crickets as no more than a single
sort of inoffensive insect, but Orientals classify a number of different species according to song—Ayako can
imitate three or four of the best known—and keep them
as pets in wonderfully-crafted little bamboo cages, feeding them bits of lettuce and cucumber. I would probably do the same except there is no need to do it; there is
always a cricket on the hearth or living somewhere in
the stonework of the chimney in the log cabin, and it
takes care of itself. I like to think it is "of the soft brown
sort / that feeds on darkness" so neatly described by
Edwin Arlington Robinson.

I have never tried the trick of measuring temperature according to cricket-song frequency—I believe the
method is accurate, but forget how the calculation is
done. I simply enjoy. There is nothing quite like lying in
bed on a calm night, reading by the mellow light of an
ancient kerosene mantle-lamp, hearing nothing beyond an infrequent loon call and the persistent cricket
song. Such peacefulness after the alarums and excur-
sions of the day cannot possibly be described in prose.
Poetry is the only way, and the closest I can come is
through a kind of bastardized *haiku* form:

> The moon peers through
> The tall pine trees
> And listens to
> A cricket sneeze.

DEER   ✻ In the good old days—the 1930s for me, but much farther back for my elders—there was an extensive and well-cared for kitchen garden at "The Pines." Bert Davis, whom I barely remember, and then John Sullivan, the hero of my childhood, planted a variety of vegetables early in the spring. Corn, peas, beets, potatoes, carrots, and so on; by the time my group usually arrived in August, they were ready. And although little kids are traditionally supposed to hate vegetables, I remember them as being delicious.✻ I also remember with particular fondness the great flood of 1934, when we paddled up and down the rows in a canoe, picking corn and beans and feeling around in the muddy water for carrots—

✻And fun. With 15 or 20 of us seated at the long, narrow porch table, Grandfather served the baked potatoes from his position at the head by the simple expedient of throwing them to everyone.

The point of all this is that it had to be protected from the deer, and so there was an extensive system of fencing. The garden itself, perhaps some 30 yards by 10 yards, was enclosed by chicken wire to keep out raccoons and rabbits. Beyond that was a heavy, open-mesh wire fence about five feet high that ran from west to east along the south of the garden, thus preventing approach through the swamp of the cove, then turned north and ran across the whole point to the shore. I never understood what was to prevent the deer from swimming around it and I still don't, because most of the northern spur remains in place. Where it was sta-pled to trees it is now ingrown three and four inches and more. The rest of the fence was beaten down by snowdrifts when the garden was abandoned after WW II, and every once in a while I would trip over it, hidden in the leaves and ferns.

Then some years ago we opened camp right after ice-out, and when a large snow drift on the edge of the garden finally melted we found a complete set of deer bones, picked clean except for a few scraps of hair and skin. The general opinion of those who should know was that a bobcat was responsible, and that may well be—but I wondered if perhaps the deer had first broken a leg in that old fence wire. So I tore it loose from the roots and dirt and rolled up as much as I could.

For the number of times deer are actually seen close to or in camp, all that fencing would hardly seem worth the trouble. But it is not necessary to go very far in any direction to know that they are around; tracks and droppings are everywhere, not to mention close-cropped tall grass, clumps of shrubbery, and occa-sionally Ayako's carefully-tended flowers. They're there all right, and those who think deer hunting is about as sporting as clubbing cattle in the stockyard don't know just how elusive deer are, even though all the signs and indications point to being surrounded by them. Per-sonally, I gave up deer hunting when I realized I was not meant for it. I lack the true killer instinct, prefer other more pleasurable ways to prove my manhood, and in the years when I did go afield with malice aforethought I found that every time I carried a deer-rifle I saw only partridge, and when I carried a shotgun I saw only deer. I got the message and quit.

DOGS * The dogs of Onawa are so varied according to size, shape, color, breed, and character that it is impossible to deal with them in general terms. The only way is to categorize them. Owner's names are omitted as necessary to protect the innocent and guilty impartially.

<u>Smallest</u>: A toss-up between a deformed Italian Greyhound which looked like something that should be sitting on a flying buttress of Notre Dame, and Grandmother's Pekinese which was much addicted to nipping ankles.

<u>Largest</u>: A gigantic Newfoundland Retriever—often mistaken for a pet bear—to whom a whole leg would be a mere appetizer.

<u>Quietest</u> (and probably best behaved): John Sullivan's Springer Spaniel, "King," which I cannot ever remember barking. Elmer Berg likes to tell how, when John came to the store, he would order King to lie down under the writing shelf by the post office window. In spite of twenty or thirty people and other dogs milling around at such times, King never moved until John told him it was time to go, even when John left the store with everyone else to meet The Scoot.

<u>Noisiest</u>: A pair of collies that barked incessantly. Never one or the other, but both. If they were mercifully silent for a few minutes, the merest suggestion of a growl or bark from one would set off the other and then they were good for an hour or more. There wasn't much wild game around when they were in residence.

<u>Most Glamorous</u>: A pair of Afghans, with a lot more character than is usually attributed to such super-aris-

·tocratic dogs. Evelyn Berblinger brought them on a visit to the Bettisons some years ago, and she spent the better part of one afternoon shampooing, clipping, combing, brushing, and grooming them until they were ready for the Westchester dog show or whatever— and ten minutes after release they were having a lovely time chasing frogs in the muddy swamp of Bettison's Cove.

In the 1930s the Collins family also had an Afghan which was a source of unending amusement and confusion. The Collins' guide was Basil Philbrook, who was beyond any doubt the most memorable of all Onawa characters. Stories about Basil are treasured like the finest gems they are, no matter how often brought out to admire. For example: I remember once going down the lake with him in the old scow. It was misty and showery, so Basil sat facing the stern while I steered the motor. It wasn't all that bad, however, and thus I made some remark to this effect. "Hell," said Basil, "I'm like an old hawg. I don't care where I'm going, I just want to see where I've been."* A whole book could be and should be written about Basil, particularly before those of us who remember him are all gone.

Mrs. Collins could not have been more different. She looked like a Gainsborough painting and had manners to match. She was a very, very gentle Quaker, and we grandchildren always had to switch to "thee" and "thou" when summoned to an audience at the tea-parties regularly held by Mrs. Collins and Grandmother.

The Afghan's name was "Fazel." Further comment is superfluous.

<u>Most Exotic</u>: Two Lhasa Apsos. "Tiger" belonged to Pat Driscoll, and although I got along with him quite well he was indiscriminate about biting everyone else including Pat's father, Alfred Driscoll, former governor of New Jersey. The only one Tiger really tolerated was Jana, Pat's Indian *amah* when her kids were small, and I always suspected that was because Jana spoke Hindi to him. They were a strange pair at Onawa.

---

*Thirty years later when, beyond the wildest dreams of either Basil or myself, I was First Assessor of Elliottsville Plantation, I used this quote as an epigraph for the 1977 Annual Report.

The other apso was "Dorje," which is Tibetan for "thunderbolt," and he was much the same even to the point of biting his owners. Lindley Bettison, his host when visiting, was fond of quoting the Governor's final dictum on Tiger: "if he gets within range, kick him."

Best Swimmer: The most unlikely dogs will swim across Onawa or even a mile and more along the length if given the opportunity and conviction that they have been abandoned, but none of them comes anywhere near the performance of "Lady." Lady was a small, beagle-like mutt that appeared from the forest one day and spent the better part of a week swimming up, down, and across the lake from one camp to another, either searching for a lost owner or inspecting possible new homes. Inquiry was made as to lost dogs, ads were placed in the *Piscataquis Observer* and the *Bangor Daily News*, but no reply was ever received. Lady was eventually adopted by Margaret Conklin, given her name, and rode out of Onawa in chauffeured luxury: a true rags-to-riches story.

Most Pathetic: My father's Laborador, "Tinker," in her old age. The last time she came to Onawa was in the '60s, when we still left cars at the Bodfish Farm and walked the old trail to Long Pond Stream. The forest and wildlife smells must have been irresistible, but every time she tried to follow a track off the path she kept running into trees, logs, and stones because she was almost blind. She would whimper a bit, get back on the trail, and plod along until something else was too good to miss—and do the same thing again. It was heartbreaking.

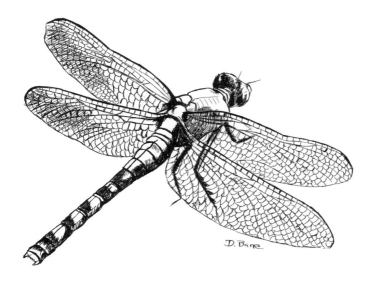

* As a one-time pilot and lifelong student of anything **DRAGONFLIES**
airborne, I am fascinated by dragonflies. The perfect
flying machines they are often called in even the most
abstruse technical literature. And they certainly are.
Fast, supremely manueverable, capable of hovering
and vertical flight, not even the hummingbird can
match the dragonfly for sheer virtuosity of flight; who
ever saw a hummingbird glide? But the dragonfly does,
on those marvelously-engineered gossamer wings. All
other insects (at least those I have observed) excepting
only the butterfly, must operate in a continuous power-
on mode if they are to remain aloft. A patrolling dragonfly spends more time gliding than under power:
true efficiency.

And, efficient and ferocious predators. The dragonfly nymph is normally referred to as a voracious
killer of mosquitoes and other underwater insect lar-
vae; I have never observed this, but there are few scenes
of such intense activity as that of a host of newly-
hatched dragonflies hunting black flies over the
swampy area of the cove. More power to them. And
when that frenzy has run its course there are few
scenes more peaceful and relaxing than sitting on the
boathouse porch on a warm, sunny, calm morning,
watching the dragonflies patrol back and forth, back
and forth, with an occasional dart to the side for a
mosquito or gnat.

Or something bigger. At one such time I was admiring a dragonfly resting motionless on the boathouse porch near my seat on the steps. I was thinking all the conventional thoughts about the wonderful grace, delicacy, and beauty of this exceptional insect when it suddenly flew off. So much for appreciation of Nature, I thought. And then, almost before I had time to raise my eyes, it was back in the same spot—with a small butterfly in its grasp, which it calmly and methodically devoured except for the wings. It's just as well those three-foot-span monsters of the carboniferous era died out.

* William Cullen Bryant did not say what sort of wa- **DUCKS**
terfowl he was referring to in his famous poem, but
internal evidence indicates that it was certainly a duck
rather than a goose, gull, heron, or other waterbird. It is
hardly surprising that he was not more specific, since
he saw the bird only in "the last steps of day . . . darkly
seen against the crimson sky . . . at that far height." In
these circumstances Peterson himself could do no
more than say it was a duck.

Nevertheless, I am willing to bet it was a black
duck, for three reasons. The first two are practical: both
Massachusetts, where Bryant lived when he wrote *To a
Waterfowl* in 1815, and central Maine are within the
year-round resident range for blacks. Also, the bird was
alone, and I have often noted that blacks tend to be
rather solitary, in marked contrast to the gregarious
mallards and many other puddle-ducks. There are not
that many ducks living around Onawa, but occasionally when exploring Flood Cove or the inlet swamp
a single duck will spring into the air from the dense
marsh-reeds—invariably a black.

The third reason is more tenuous, and yet the most
convincing of all; I had much the same experience as
Bryant, though I did not think of it that way at the
time. Indeed, I did not think of Bryant at all until long
afterwards.

One calm, cool evening in early fall, Ayako and I
decided to give the fishing a final try just at sundown.
We were both tired and didn't want to bother with the
usual routine of loading all the fishing gear into a
boat,so we thought we would simply do a bit of spin-
casting off the stone-throwing beach and admire the
sunset at the same time. I went to the boathouse, then,
to get our spinning rods, and while there I noted a
single black duck slowly paddling along the shoreline
of the cove toward the boathouse. Nothing unusual
about that, if a bit late. I waited quietly until it had
passed, then went up to the kitchen with the rods and
from there to the stone-throwing beach on the north

shore. We had been fishing for some minutes without saying anything to each other—just casting and retrieving with no real expectations—when the black duck came silently around the point. We both stood motionless as the duck paddled by about ten feet offshore and disappeared behind the big boulders at the pumphouse beach.

The light was fading, but the fish were beginning to rise, and we thought there might be a chance for something out on the back point, where we have infrequently taken trout and salmon at such times. We walked the woods trail out back, took up position on the boulders, made a few casts—and the black duck appeared again, this time closer to shore than ever, carefully investigating each nook and cranny among the jumbled rocks as it moved slowly along. It passed almost under my feet, equally close to Ayako, then out of sight around the boulders at the entrance to the back cove. All this in silence, in the last light of an infinitely peaceful sunset.

The black was looking for a safe place to spend the night, and I thought of all that implied: the foxes, minks, snapping turtles, bobcats, and other deadly menaces. I thought of the weather; it was going to be a cold night. Suddenly, I had an overwhelming understanding of what a wild creature was up against, and a fiercely protective urge similar to what one would feel for an old and faithful dog—and at the same time I knew I could do nothing. It was a strange mixture of vast sympathy and frustration and something like love for all living things in the wild.

To Bryant the waterfowl disappearing into the sunset was a mystical, didactic experience:

> He who, from zone to zone
> Guides through the boundless day thy certain
>   flight,
> In the long way that I must tread alone
> Will lead my steps aright.

Not having a Puritan turn of mind I did not see it in quite the same manner, but it affected me just as deeply. While battlefield relations are all very dramatic, insignificant incidents can carry every bit as much meaning and understanding.

EAGLES

∗ Eagles are even bigger and more impressive birds than you think they are. And the term "eagle-eye" means a lot more than mere visual acuity; you have no idea what it is all about until you have had an eagle *really* look at you. I have never gotten over the time we were driving north along the Chilkat River, from Haynes and Port Chilkoot in Alaska back to Teslin in the Yukon Territory. We spotted an eagle sitting in the top of a dead tree next to the road, and hoping not to disturb it drove by for perhaps a quarter of a mile before stopping. As we walked slowly back the eagle turned its attention from the river to us. Even from a distance I felt uncomfortable under that unwavering stare, and at our closest approach—some 50 feet from the tree—I was transfixed. Full-grown with pure white head and tail, sitting majestically aloft and staring down at me; the effect was awesome. That great golden eye examined my inmost thoughts, dissected my very soul, and it was all I could do to keep from falling to my knees and confessing everything I could think of and inventing sins I had never committed. Years later I found much to puzzle over while reading *The Divine Comedy*, but the passage concerning Minos and his judgment process was instantly familiar. I knew exactly what Dante was talking about.

Around Onawa I have never had that close a look at an eagle, and I am not sure I want to. They soar far overhead occasionally, and every other year or so there is a rumor that a pair are nesting somewhere up in Flood Cove, but I have never seen either the eagles or their nest, so I doubt it. In fact the only one I have seen other than in flight was sitting in the very top of the tallest of the great old white pines on the back point. It was first noticed by guests arriving for our new-boathouse party in 1972—a real blast involving the whole lake that is still talked about—and seemed a particularly happy omen under the circumstances. Eagles are like that; it is no wonder they are so symbolic in all cultures and times.

* Eels are one of those viands (not food, *viands*) that **EELS** medieval kings used to die of a surfeit of, and this is understandable—they had varlets (not servants) to take the eels off the hook and clean them. Wrapped in foil and broiled over coals, eel-meat is pure white, tender, and delicious; there is not much better to eat. And not much worse to kill and clean. Or so I have always understood and fully believe in spite of never having attempted it myself. Although not particularly squeamish about cleaning other fish, and not in the least bothered by the snakelike aspect which disturbs many men and absolutely horrifies women, there is something singularly revolting about that slimy, prehistoric *thing* tying itself in knots as it writhes on the end of the line. It may be my own peculiar hang-up, or it may be a billion-year-old racial memory of times when an eel, or something like it, was a deadly enemy—and having observed many times how aggressively the eels snap up the results of fish-cleaning at the end of the dock, I am inclined to favor the latter theory. I don't care; even knowing how good they are to eat I will still cut the line rather than clean one. Ugh.

FIREFLIES   * Fireflies are highly improbable creatures when you think about it. If they didn't already exist, they are the sort of exotic, alien life-form that might be expected in good science-fiction—or that NASA hoped would show up in the first photos from the Viking lander on Mars. After all, what could be more unlikely than a small, easily-caught flying beetle that will wander about your hand waving its long antennae in peaceful curiosity— and then suddenly light up its whole rear end like a tiny fluorescent tube?

Natural phosphorescence is always more than a bit weird, so why is it that the will-o'-the-wisp, *ignis fatuus*, swamp gas, or whatever you want to call it is regarded with so much superstitious awe while the firefly is considered in no way unusual? There is familiarity of course, in this case breeding not contempt but merely indifference, yet the real reason is a lot simpler: on a warm summer evening the swamp in the cove is filled with little noises—crickets, lapping water, peepers, the infrequent cry of a sleepy bird—and over all this tranquillity ephemeral sparks of light hover and swing in graceful arabesques. How could such loveliness possibly be regarded as sinister?

D. Bane

✻ Fishers are rarely seen around Onawa, but we always know when one has been in the area: no red squirrels. At least that is the reason given by the local woodsmen whenever there is a complete disappearance of red squirrels. It seems likely enough. Seton wrote that only the marten can catch a squirrel, and only a fisher can catch a marten. Peterson's *Field Guide to the Mammals* notes that "the fisher is more at home in the trees than it is on the ground." So while it may well be that the red squirrels are cleaned out by martens, it is just as likely that the fisher is responsible and the local trappers' theory—undoubtedly handed down through many generations—is correct.

Whatever, they must be fearsome little animals. In 1967 in the Yukon Territory I saw a caged marten. It was beautiful, but infinitely more impressive than the rich coat was its voice. From something that small you don't expect much; a high-pitched yipping or squealing. Not at all. It grasped the cage wires, bared a set of murderous teeth, and emitted a deep, throaty, resonant

The Onawa Bestiary   **43**

growl that was bone-chilling in its elemental ferocity. Since the fisher is a close relative and even bigger, I think I would rather face an angry bear—well, bobcat, anyway. Particularly since they are also smart enough to be the only animals capable of killing a porcupine without getting full of quills.

Only once did we see a fisher, if that is what it was. Coming around the point in a small boat I saw it hunting along the rocks of the shoreline. Lithe, sinuous, with bushy tail and very dark fur, it was much too big for a mink and not heavy enough for an otter. By the time I docked the boat and ran to the area it was gone. As I remember, there were no red squirrels that year.

* Being what they are—very nocturnal and very **FLYING**
quiet—it is very hard to know if flying squirrels are **SQUIRRELS**
around or not. Exactly the opposite of red squirrels,
which cannot possibly be missed. Only twice have I
seen a flying squirrel, and I am not so sure about the
first time. All I know is that as I stood on the boathouse
porch admiring the moonlit scene in the cove, something glided rapidly across the sky to my left, from high
in the big pines back of the boathouse to a low clump of
maples on the edge of the cove. It certainly wasn't a
bat, and it didn't have the right feeling—for lack of a
better term—for a bird, even with partially folded
wings.

The Onawa Bestiary **45**

The second time it was unmistakable. Late at night in the log cabin we heard a persistent scratching like that of a mouse, only a bit stronger, from the area of the eaves close to the chimney. Flashlight in hand, I searched and found nothing inside. Since the scratching persisted it had to be outside, so I looked through the tiny bathroom window that opens onto the same area. There, perched on a shoulder of the chimney just under the eaves, was a flying squirrel. With its rich gray-brown fur above sharply differentiated from the pure white belly by the loose folds of skin along the sides, and the huge liquid eyes, I have never seen anything that conveyed such a feeling of softness. An angora rabbit skin or a handful of goose down seemed like a bag of nails in comparison. I would have given much to see it spread those membranes and leap away, but it was frozen in the light. So we went back to bed and heard no more scratching.

D. Bane

* Foxes come and go in cycles that depend on the   **FOXES**
abundance of rabbits, according to theory. I have no
way to prove or disprove this, but neither do I much
doubt it. Certainly they are common some years, then
seemingly extinct during others. Throughout one two-
week vacation in the middle '60s we saw more foxes
around Onawa than all other times put together.

There was one digging for turtle eggs on the sand
beach as we paddled by in a canoe. It may have been
the same fox or another that we saw on the gravel-cliff
slightly to the north a few days later. Foxes ran across
the road as we drove in and out from Monson, and once
on the way to Greenville we saw a fox sitting at the
upper end of an open field near Indian Hill, watching
with interest the road crew as they cleared the ditch. I
was reminded of an incident related by Darwin:

> In the evening we reached the island of San
> Pedro, where we found the *Beagle* at anchor. In
> doubling the point, two of the officers landed to

take a second round of angles with the theolodite. A fox (*canis fulvipes*) of a kind said to be peculiar to the island, and very rare in it, and which is a new species, was sitting on the rocks. He was so intently absorbed in watching the officers, that I was able, by quietly walking up behind, to knock him on the head with my geological hammer. This fox, more curious or more scientific, but less wise, than the generality of his brethren, is now mounted in the museum of the Zoological Society.*

Most wonderful of all, however, was the day we were having lunch on the south porch. There were my mother and father, Ayako and I, Terris and Katrina Moore, and Terris' expatriate sister Karleen and her English husband, Cecil Pim, who did not invent the Pimm's Cup but might well have. Old Bill Easton, the cook, was in the kitchen. It was not a particularly noisy party, but neither was it very quiet. So the amazement was general when I left the porch for the kitchen and quickly reported back that a vixen and two kits were coming along the path from the old garden. She approached cautiously but without any real hesitation. The kits followed a few feet behind until reaching the edge of the kitchen porch; then they ran down onto the lawn below the south porch and began playing. Slowly and with much sniffing of the rich kitchen odors (Bill was cooking one of his incomparable chicken pies) the vixen walked onto the porch and neared the kitchen door. Bill opened the screen door and stood motionless, holding out something in the natural gesture of offering to a pet. She came to within a few feet of Bill, then decided either that she did not like the offering, or that the whole affair was getting out of hand, turned, and ran down the steps to the lawn where the kits were falling all over each other with joyous abandon. She joined in this play for a few moments as we all watched spellbound, then led them off into the shrubbery by the boathouse. Bill was a taciturn, even morose, old man and it was some time before he would admit he had been feeding the vixen for days.

---

*Charles Darwin, *The Voyage of the Beagle*, Bantam Books, New York, NY, 1958. p 241.

So it was that kind of a year for foxes; the theory held true for all respects including that of disease-vectors. As we departed for Buffalo we had driven up the road from Bodfish Farm (where we left the car in those days) no more than a quarter of a mile when we saw a fox lying at the side of the road, watching the car approach with no interest whatsoever. I stopped beside it and saw at once why it took no alarm; it was was one of the most miserable animals I have ever seen. Thin, mangey, with ragged coat and bleary eyes, it was far beyond caring about anything but whatever warmth it could soak up in the sunlight. If my .22 had not been packed so deeply I would have shot it as an act of mercy.

FROGS ✱ It is hardly an original observation, but there is something inherently comical about frogs, particularly the common bullfrog, and this is something to wonder about. The bug-eyed aspect is obvious and somehow ridiculous, and the deep, resonant voice of such a small animal is certainly incongruous and hence amusing in that respect. The real source of comedy, however, most probably lies in the frog's enormous dignity. Ponderous, unsmiling, supercilious, the frog sits there like the object of so many classic satires: the clerk, the bureaucrat, the high prelate, the magistrate—everything that is filled with pompous self-importance. And then in the most carefree and juvenile of all actions it suddenly jumps a remarkable distance—still grim and unsmiling. Again, it is the contrast, the incongruity. One would have to go deep into the philosophy of humor to know just *why* this is so amusing, but it is.

At all events, frogs are certainly the favorites of small boys and dogs. I put in my time catching frogs in the cove, and every small boy that has ever come to camp has done the same. Dogs don't really seem to care whether or not they actually catch anything— they simply have a glorious time wading around the swamp in pursuit. Tinker, our Laborador, would spend all day doing this, although she never caught a frog. Ginger, the Burns' springer spaniel, patrolled the sand beach in like manner. Lindley Bettison claimed that even when she found a frog she just "breathed on it" and I saw her doing something very much like that at times. She stood in the water, tail wagging furiously,

with open mouth barely above the surface, breathing heavily. Very odd.

"Frogs," according to one of my books on wilderness survival, "are very tenacious of life." I will guarantee that. Long ago, my father and I used to shoot frogs in the inlet swamp, and I remember all too vividly how a frog even with most of its head blown off had to be stabbed again and again. It was messy, as was the cutting-off and cleaning of legs. But good. And another case of "the good old days," or at least of a changing ecology. Some years ago Ayako and I went frog-hunting in the same area. There were plenty of frogs, but none of them even close to eating size. I cannot imagine why.

What we need is a whole swamp full of frogs the size of Big George, who lives under the dock. Big George is the patriarch of them all; about the size of that frog featured in the ads proclaiming that you too can raise frogs for fun and profit. His voice is prodigious when he announces himself, and so are his legs. But like the woodcock in the old garden there is only one of him per year, and so we leave him alone. Besides which, I figure that being the size he is he must eat an awful lot of mosquitoes and black flies. Then too, he is frequently good for a laugh during a lull in the conversation—the burp at the dinner party and that sort of thing. He's worth more as a character than as a pair of legs.

If a full-grown frog presents a generally lean and well-muscled appearance, surely the tadpole is the ultimate example of being overstuffed. To observe one at rest, rocking gently with the water motion, eyes popping from skin as tight as a ripe grape and tiny full-lipped mouth gasping, is to remember exactly the engorged aftermath of a staggering thanksgiving feast. Because of what is going on inside with all those legs trying to get out while the tail is trying to get back in, perhaps the tadpole feels that way too. In this respect the tadpole is more interesting than the frog. There are few such examples of metamorphosis. The caterpillar retires to a cocoon for the well-nigh unbelievable transformation to a butterfly, and the dragonfly emerges full-grown from the nymph shell. Nothing is seen of the complete re-design of a living creature. But the tadpole makes the change right there in the shallow, warm water of the swampy areas, in full view of anyone with the patience to observe. Legs appear and grow; the eyes move to the top of the head; the mouth widens and the gills fade away; the tail shortens—week by week and month by month the metamorphosis proceeds, and what began as a jelly bean with a tail ends as a frog.

* Gulls are seashore birds, flying tourist-traps having **GULLS**
nothing to do with Onawa:

> Black-tipped white wheeling wings belong
> With a hissing surf and broken shells
> Sidewise tenlegs and seaweed smells
> On the salty gale that combs the hair
> Back from the brow of the sand dune where
> An unseen bird pipes a reedy song—
>
> Not here, in the land of the loon
> And the crystalline mountain stream

Nevertheless, the few that hang around Onawa seem a lot more natural than the hundreds that infest small-town dumps—or the thousands wheeling about the vast garbage-mountains of the Jersey marshlands between the George Washington Bridge and the turn-pike—sounding like a slow freight creaking over a very bad track. With a load of rusty hinges.

Spotless white, softest gray, accented with black, the symbol of all that is clean and fresh and unspoiled along the wide world's shoreline, soaring with such matchless grace and ease; how can they have such disgusting taste? They're scavengers, of course, but they ought to look the part, like vultures and buzzards. Dump eagles, Bill Allen calls them, and he's right. There's a moral there, but it doesn't bear thinking about for very long.

D. Bane

HARES ✳ Around Onawa, there are plenty of snowshoe hares. They bound away through the woods on occasion, and I frequently wonder that we do not see more of them since their droppings are everywhere. Out in the woods they are apparently as timid as their reputation credits them, but around camp just the opposite. There is usually at least one living in the area, more rarely two. Or at least we only see one. We always call it "Bigfoot," for obvious reasons. When foraging on the lawn in front of the big camp or along the other pathways, it will allow us to approach within a few feet before loping away in no great hurry. When it is established that we mean no harm, Bigfoot pays as little attention to our comings and goings as we do to his.

Why should we? Unlike the cutesy-cuddly cottontail, the snowshoe hare is not all that attractive. With huge hind feet and ears, it is rather lean and stringy-looking even when well-fed later in the year. In the spring when they are changing color they have a ragged, diseased sort of look—mottled with irregular splotches of winter white and summer brown—that is singularly unappetizing whenever I look at one as a possible dinner.

So we leave them alone. About the only way I would consider them as game would be to hunt according to the rules of Elmer Berg and Basil Philbrook: go in deep mid-winter, heavily clothed and on snowshoes, armed with nothing bigger than a .22 pistol. If that isn't a sporting chance for a fast and elusive quarry, I don't know what it is. It's a good alternative to cabin fever.

A Ballade of Cabin Fever*

I study the pictures hung on the wall,
Remark the design of the rug on the floor,
Wander again down the cold, drafty hall
Glaring in mirrors, slamming the door,
Stare out the window and wonder what
    more,
How much more snow can it possibly bring;
This unending winter. O God! What a bore!
How long is it yet until spring?

Darkness descends like a funeral pall;
I listen with hate to the furnace's roar;
Tomorrow the oil-man is coming to call;
Even the thought makes my blood-pressure
    soar
As I note that the windows are painted with
    hoar.
Life has become an unraveling string,
And ever and ever again I implore
How long is it yet until spring?

When the mildest remark is unbearable gall
And my vision is stained with blood and
    with gore,
It is only too clear what I need is a brawl,
A weekend more lost than any before;
A wall-banging riot to even the score,
A chair-busting, free-swinging, wild sort of
    thing.
When will it end? Will it never be o'er?
How long is it yet until spring?

   L'envoi
Prince, I know I am mad as I roar
But at this time of year, how can I sing?
My soul is chilled to its innermost core;
How long is it yet until spring?

---

*Reprinted by permission of *The Bangor Daily News*

HAWKS ✻ There are many hawks around Onawa, but whether they are red-tailed, red-shouldered, broad-winged, sharp-shinned, or whatever is damned hard to tell. Peterson's "confusing fall warblers" are bad enough; although far larger birds, hawks are much worse because of their natural camouflage and the greater distance at which they are usually seen. For the most part, if such a bird is soaring overhead I note the wingtips—broad or pointed—classify it as either a hawk or falcon, and let it go at that.

The only one I was ever really sure of was not a hawk, strictly speaking, but a falcon: a pigeon hawk. Driving to Monson one day, we found it lying in the road not far from James Brook. It had not been shot, run over, or damaged in any way; it was simply dead. It was also beautiful and would look magnificent on the big-camp mantelpiece. So we took it straight to the warden in Guilford and asked about a permit to have it mounted. He knew nothing about that—only that it would be noted and then "disposed of." Horrified at the idea of such a gorgeous thing being thrown out with the garbage, I wrote to the then head of the Fish and Wildlife Service in Augusta. (Long ago I learned that top-echelon people are frequently more responsive where those of the lower levels are not. My father once got a permit to have mounted an accidentally-shot wood duck, approved and signed by the terrible-tempered Mr. Ickes himself, then Secretary of the Interior.) I received a surprisingly quick, courteous, and informative answer. Along with thanking me for saving the

D. Bane

bird, the letter went on to explain that the warden I spoke to was not aware that such birds, in good condition, are given to museums and universities requesting them for study and display. Thus, researchers do not have to kill a live bird, and the bird found dead is put to good use. The hawk in question had already been transferred from the warden's freezer to the government's, and would be given to a qualified institution.

A minor matter, but it made me feel a whole lot better about the situation. And Augusta. If all government agencies were run by men like that, how wonderful it would be—

The Onawa Bestiary   **57**

HUMMINGBIRDS   * The usual thing with hummingbirds is to "Oooooooh" and "Aaaaaah" about them as if they were particularly beautiful babies. Such gorgeous little creatures, sweet and delicate and all that is rosy-hued—or in this case, ruby-throated—fluttering long, long lashes over huge liquid eyes while sipping nectar from eager-to-give flowers as syrupy chords are plucked on the heartstrings. Nature at its most benign and benevolent, squared and cubed.

Hardly. Hummingbirds are certainly beautiful and their powers of flight are unique, but otherwise they are about as sweet and gentle as a Tiger tank. Alice Moore keeps three or four hummingbird feeders in front of her porch, and on a summer afternoon one can sit peacefully and quietly and still be exhausted just watching the frantic activity of the hummingbirds at their most aggressive-possessive. It is hard to tell how many there are altogether, but four or six can be seen at any one time, each claiming exclusive rights to not one feeder but all of them. Any given bird gets no more than a couple of seconds at a feeder before it must chase off two or three others. It is no matter that the others have gone to feeders several feet distant; they are not permitted to encroach on this gold mine of nectar, to mix a metaphor along with the sugar and water. The result is that none of them gets much of anything. Indeed, if you want to think in terms of the energy equation, it seems probable that there is a net loss; more energy is expended in defending the source than is acquired from it. Instinct does not always work for the common, or individual good.

Hummingbirds also tend to be impatient when it is

feeding time. There is nothing unusual about having one hover nearby while I re-fill our own feeder, but the first hummingbird that showed up in the spring of 1986 was something else when it arrived early and the feeder was not out. The bird hovered in front of the kitchen picture-window, skidding a bit from side to side, looking into the interior where Ayako and I sat at the table. At first this seemed mere curiosity, but as the moments passed it became obvious the bird was expecting something. It remembered. So I took the feeder from the winter-storage hook on the wall and went out onto the porch to hang it in its usual place from a branch of the white pine the chipmunks use to scramble up and jump onto the porch. The hummingbird disappeared. But as I filled the feeder the bird was back, so impatient it hovered within inches of my hands. "OK. OK, take it easy," I said. "Here. You want a drink?" I held out the feeder. The bird immediately moved in and began to drink. When a hummingbird is hungry it expects to be fed, *und schnell!* A few minutes later it chased away a chickadee that had come to a nearby feeder full of sunflower seeds.

KINGFISHERS *   —After the kingfisher's wing
Has answered light to light, and is silent, the light
is still
At the still point of the turning world.*

Exactly what T. S. Eliot is talking about in this passage from the *Burnt Norton* section of his *Four Quartets* is highly debatable, but it is also a good, if extremely stylized, description of the flight of a kingfisher. The kingfisher's sudden flight from tree to tree along an otherwise tranquil shoreline or stream bank has the effect of intensifying the scene. This is partly due to the loud, bucket-of-bolts rattle invariably uttered at such time, but even more to the brilliant blue-and-white wingbeat against the brown and green foliage. The colors of sky and cloud, the king-fisher's wing indeed answers light to light, and when the bird perches again it becomes a motionless point of color in a subdued setting.

Much of the power and genius of Eliot's poetry rests on his technique of contrasting the artificiality of city life with unspoiled nature, and his nature-images are startling in their vividness. So Eliot may have been the supremely intellectual poet of The Hollow Men living in The Waste Land, but he also understood kingfishers.

The Collected Poems of T. S. Eliot, 1909 - 1935, Harcourt Brace and Company, New York, NY 1936.

✳ To see a loon in flight is to be mildly surprised; they **LOONS** are so much a part of the water-scenery that it is easy to forget they are actually birds. The black ducks that live around the lake, the flocks of old-squaw, buffle-head, golden-eye, and other puddle-ducks that migrate through in the fall; all these are very shy and at the least alarm will leap into the air in a wondrous confu-sion of wings and water. Even the Sheldrake will begin a long, fast, take-off run using full power of both feet and *wings*. But if you get too close to a loon it simply dives, like a muskrat, beaver, frog, or any other water animal. It seems likely that in the long run loons will evolve into something much like the penguin: an ex-pert under-water swimmer that is clumsy on land and incapable of flight.

Watching a loon take off makes it clear why they really don't like to fly. If a Sheldrake makes a long take-off run at least it seems in character since the Sheldrake rarely flies higher than a few feet off the water anyway. But a loon flies at something more like a normal altitude, and to get there involves an agoniz-ingly long, water-slapping take-off and a lot of slow climbing in wide circles. The effort must seem hardly worth it. No wonder the loon has that hunchbacked appearance in flight—it's tired. And since the fishing in the next lake is probably no better than in Onawa, why bother? So loons rarely fly, and don't approve much of things that do. Other birds they treat with dignified contempt, ignoring them. Airplanes are another mat-

D. Bane

ter. The high-flying jets don't seem to bother them, but a bush plane that comes anywhere near the lake will invariably bring forth a whole chorus of indignant calls.

This seems rather curious. There are plenty of other man-noises and irritations around the lake—pump engines, the CPRR trains, occasional shooting, and most intrusive of all, outboard-powered boats. None of this disturbs the loons. A boat can be driven within 20 yards of a loon and most of the time it will do nothing more than dive, and sometimes not even that. But a light plane so far distant or high as to be barely audible will start them off. Interesting.

Another odd, un-birdlike thing about loons is the blackness of their head feathers. It is a flat, non-reflecting black that might well be the definition of the word "black." Peterson describes the head and neck as "glossy black," but I dispute this. I have studied too many loons with a telescope and had many more surface close to my fishing boat, and that black is in no way glossy. Black birds of every kind from redwings to ravens have a certain gloss or iridescence when seen in strong sunlight, but not the loon. Not around Onawa in summertime, anyway; a loon's head is the elemental blackness of interstellar space, absorbing all light and reflecting none. To me, at least, it is disturbing, and even a bit eerie—

Loon chicks are brownish-black little balls of fluff, also non-reflective, and it may take a moment to realize what it is you are looking at when spotting a couple riding on their mother's back, particularly if the mother is operating at near periscope-depth. Loons seem able to control their flotation far more closely than most water birds. Ducks and geese float high and dry unless actually tipping up, but a loon is just as likely to swim along with the body completely awash and only the neck and head above water—which makes a lot of sense in windy, rough-water conditions. On days so windy that nothing else is on the lake, the loons will be sailing along from trough to crest, not in the least dismayed. In the old Navy when a submarine was a surface vessel that also had diving capability, I believe they submerged in rough weather for exactly the same reason; you can go about your business without fighting the wind and waves.

Loon chicks are also interesting in having a definite limit to their fish-capacity, where the adults seemingly have none. It is a wonderfully amusing study in bafflement to watch a pair of loons trying to feed a chick that is full. They will swim to the chick with minnow in beak, offer it again and again and be repeatedly refused. They move away, circle around, try again, and are again refused. After half a dozen or more repetitions of this performance they will eat the minnows themselves, dive for more, and start the whole act all over again. It is incomprehensible that the chick does not want more, and risky as it is to attribute human emotions to animals it is impossible not to sympathize with the frustration so evident in feeding a recalcitrant child.

Another proof of the loon's total commitment to water is their extreme awkwardness on land. Other water birds manage to get about well enough, if none too gracefully, in the duck-walk waddle they originated, but a loon doesn't come even close to this degree of mobility. More than anything a loon pushes itself around on its belly, sliding on the wet marsh-vegetation or sand. Even on land, they swim. At least that is the

way I remember it the one time I saw a loon on land—
and it was a heart-breaking example of natural selec-
tion as well. Ordinarily the loons nest far back in Duck
Cove, the Inlet marsh, and other isolated areas of the
shoreline where the eggs can be well hidden. But this
loon had laid her two eggs on the sandy beach of the
little island just off our point, with no more covering
than a few alder branches, and a pair of ravens discovered them at once. So it became a waiting game. The
ravens sat on boulders to either side of the tiny beach;
the loon sat in the middle, guarding her eggs and
looking from one raven to the other. One raven at a
time could go for other food, but the loon could not, and
she must have become very hungry. This went on for
several days until finally hunger won out, and first one
egg was broken, then the other, and the actors in this
natural tragedy—if such a thing is possible in Nature—
disappeared.

But if tragedy in Nature is possible, then so is
comedy. There was the time when, standing on a rock
west of the Stone-Throwing Beach, I looked uplake to
the inlet and the sunset—all was tranquil, motionless
and silent. Suddenly there was a strong roil and swirl of
water a few yards to my left. What the hell was that?
Beaver? Startled beavers always slap their tails before
diving. Fish? If so, it must be the biggest ever in
Onawa. A loon? A moment later a big loon surfaced a
little farther out. It regarded me warily for a few moments, then settled into its dip-and-look routine.
Stretched, rose half out of the water, beat its wings,
settled itself. Dip-and-look. Paddle along. More dip-and-
look. And then a violent thrashing about; wings and
water exploding; panic! A loon cannot take off straight
up like a puddle-duck, but this one was certainly trying. I stared, too surprised to even wonder what was
happening, when another loon surfaced immediately
alongside the first. I still wonder if the second loon
came up under the first by accident—or had a sense of
humor.

As for the loon's call, either the long, mournful wail
or the hysterical laugh, it is the very heart and soul of
the northern lakes, and if you didn't understand that
you probably wouldn't be reading this.

D. Bane

* Like chipmunks and small birds, the deer mice **MICE**
around camp surely live in a different time dimension. I
have watched them many nights as they vacuum
clean the kitchen porch where I throw out birdseed
during the day, and it is impossible to see one actually
move. They are instantaneously here, there, somewhere else, or gone. If a family of Sheldrake look like a
speeded-up Keystone Kops movie, then the mice act
like something from the early space program where the
films were shot at one frame per two seconds. The
resultant flickering motion is very disconcerting—
rather alien, even. Mice move in normal time only
when something is wrong, like the one that slowly and
aimlessly wandered among the tools and scraps of
wood on the boathouse work-bench. It paid no attention when I offered some crumbs of the stale bread kept
nearby for chumming minnows. Eventually, it huddled
between two jars of nails and died.

The Onawa Bestiary **65**

There is really no defense against mice in an old camp like The Pines, and I long ago gave up any attempts at mouse-proofing other than the kitchen and big-camp bathroom. Aside from the unsanitary aspects of mouse turd all over the washstand shelf and chewed-up soap, it was getting silly when the mice began using the toilet paper roll for a treadmill, or log-rolling contest. A couple of yards of paper on the floor in the morning came to be normal, and several times they ran off a whole roll.

Even sillier was the mouse in the kitchen wastebasket. One calm, quiet summer evening when all doors were open, as we sat in the big-camp living room we could hear an oddly rhythmical rustling in the kitchen. Stealthy investigation with a flashlight proved this to be coming from the plastic wastebasket under the sink. A deer mouse had gotten in by way of a table-leg and was trying to get out. It would poise on a wad of crumpled paper, leap about halfway to the rim, claw frantically against the smooth side, and fall back. Again and again and again, regular as clockwork. The idea of wringing its neck or flattening it with a frying pan did not much appeal, so we dumped it on the porch and went back to the living room. An hour later it was back. We dumped it again and went to bed.

Ayako turned it out of the wastebasket next morning, and it was back again that night. So this time we painted it with a spot of bright red nail polish for positive identification and dumped it way down in the old garden. Fifteen minutes later it was back, the red spot looking a bit chewed. We took it to the edge of the swamp at the narrow neck of land that connects the point to the mainland. Within an hour it was back in the wastebasket, jumping up and falling back, jumping and falling, up and down. We threw it out and gave up. This sort of thing went on for several days until the mouse disappeared—and then reappeared three days later on the old croquet court, dead. Probably of over-exercise.

Finally, aside from the $40 worth of arctic char Sam Aertker and I caught and sold to the motel at Teslin in the Yukon Territory (does this make me a professional fisherman?), mice are the only animals that have ever made any money for me. While attending the University of Maine Graduate College in 1976 I

won the Carter Poetry Prize. The honor was very grat-
ifying, and the cash even more so. The poem was
actually written in the mid-1960s, during a dull day at
Cornell Aeronautical Laboratory in Buffalo, N.Y., where
I then worked.

A Matter of Scale

I still think it's a hell of a way
To die, and don't give me a lot of
Crap about being tender-hearted:
Suppose that it had been a lion,
That noble beast of heraldry,
Trapped in some abandoned quarry
With walls too steep for clawing up;
Then you would call it tragedy
And rend my heart with outrage for
The careless works of man—
Sure. But it was nothing so heroic:
There among the debris of
The boathouse loft; the greasy
Outboard motor parts, the rusty
Screens and broken shutters,
Worn-out lamps and lumber scraps,
Old brass beds and blistered chairs,
Standing in a cobwebbed corner
With no stopper, there I found
An antique cider-jug, and when
I blew away a quarter inch of dust
And held it to the light I saw
A deer-mouse mummy lying in
The green-stained base, dry and
Dessicated as any royal demi-god
From the Valley of the Kings.

D. Bow

MINK ✱ Several times a year we see a mink prowling along the shoreline rocks, sinuous as a snake, beautiful in its rich fur and elemental intensity. There is something all too ordinary and even domestic about a raccoon raiding the garbage can, but a hunting mink is a deadly serious affair. Two incidents stand out in memory.

The first time I ever saw a mink was in late October of the year Pope Paul first visited the U. S., early in the 1960s. I know it was that year because a few hours after the incident I watched the Pope on TV in the dilapidated old garage or shed that was laughingly called an airport terminal for civilian traffic (SAC and the B-52s were still there) at Dow Field, Bangor, in those days. The Pope was having a lot of trouble trying to conduct mass in Yankee Stadium while the wind blew his robes about wildly. It was the same major storm system that had reached New England that day, and Ayako and I were apprehensive about returning to Buffalo after having flown in for a long weekend with my parents.

In New York the storm was fading away, but at

Onawa it was a roaring northwest gale, with waves as big as any I have ever seen or want to see on the lake. (How we actually got out is another story altogether.) And snow, to my amazement; I had never been at Onawa late enough for snow. So in the course of making ready to leave I took a load of baggage to the dock, and having put it in the boat stood there admiring the scene in the cove. The bare trees, the withered ferns and marsh-grass, the snow dusting the rocks—a complete transformation of a familiar summer setting. Then something moved on the rocks about 20 feet east of the ramp: a mink. It hunted on toward the west, then, almost at the edge of the ramp, stopped and studied me for a moment before moving under the ramp, then on along the rocks around the point. Apparently I was not considered a threat. But rarely have I felt such an intruder. It was long since time we summer-people were gone and the lake reverted to the wilderness of winter; if the weather made that all too clear then the hunting mink was like hammering a brazen gong for closing time—

The other incident took place ten or a dozen years later, at almost the same spot. I was sitting on the corner of the boathouse porch one warm, sunny, calm day in August. I was cleaning a disassembled carburetor, and since this is a matter of some delicacy was quiet, making no noise and moving scarcely at all. Concentrating on the work, I was conscious of nothing but the usual bird calls and an occasional croak from Big George, the huge bull frog living under the dock. Suddenly, there was an agonizing, high-pitched squeal from the left, seemingly right at my elbow. On the path through the tall bracken and scrub willow that leads to the little beach in the cove, no more than 15 feet from me, there was a struggling, rolling ball of gray, white, and brown fur. The cries weakened, the violent thrashing-about subsided, the fur-ball began to untangle itself, and I saw that a mink had a small rabbit by the back of the neck and was killing it. When the screaming and struggling ceased and the rabbit was obviously dead, the mink dragged it down the nearest of the many runway-tunnels that opened onto the path, never releasing that death grip for an instant. I sat stunned and shaken for some minutes before resuming work.

D. Bane

MOOSE ✳ Moose are anything but a novelty around Onawa,
yet everyone knows of the latest activity.

"Seen the big moose over to Deadman's Cove?"

"Eyah. Had to follow the damn thing down the
road near half a mile yesterday before it'ud let me by."

I have been in this situation many times and have
concluded that it is not a case of being stubborn or
ornery; it is simply that moose believe roads were made
for *them*, not cars. Coming around the bend and finding the road blocked by a moose is like dealing with a
real case-hardened bureaucrat; eventually you may get
by, but first you must endure a lot of lordly indifference.
There is nothing quite as supercilious as a large moose
standing in the road, staring at your car—and there is
little to do but wait until you are permitted to use that
personal, private moose-road. On the other hand that
attitude cuts no ice with the CPRR; once every few
years a moose gets itself killed on the tracks, and after
proper investigation by the local game warden there is
feasting among the natives. And very good meat it is,
although I see nothing exceptional about it.

Moose also feel they have the right to inquire about
what is going on anytime, anywhere. Alfred Burke was

once having a peaceful supper when a young bull thrust his head in at a window, looked around, and withdrew only when Alfred whacked it across the nose with a folded newspaper. "God, but she homely," was his comment. The same sort of thing happened at The Pines in the summer of 1974. Elmer Berg and I were rebuilding the back room of the little sleeping-cabin, which was badly damaged when a big pine broke off and fell across it during a violent windstorm the previous winter. Elmer always arrived very early, frequently before I was fully operational, and one morning he and Ayako were drinking coffee in the kitchen when Ayako heard a step on the porch, looked up expecting to see me, and saw instead a young moose! The moose had taken several more steps along the porch by the time Elmer joined Ayako at the door, then stopped and stared at them as Elmer began to laugh and Ayako yelled at me to look out the window. In the log cabin I was up and mostly dressed by this time but by no means fully awake, and since Ayako had not specified which window I went to the nearest one, facing north. Nothing unusual there. I was puzzling over this while Elmer laughed and Ayako yelled when suddenly the whole seventh cavalry went charging down the path on the south side of the cabin. Or so it sounded. It was a hell of a way to wake up.

So I didn't see that moose, but later that fall I saw a far more impressive one in a spectacular setting, and learned something else besides. Partridge hunting along the Barren road, Ayako and I had been following moose tracks for some distance. The tracks were obviously fresh, and as we moved along they began to look fresher all the time. I studied the tracks in a sandy area; the undercut ridges of sand at the edge had not even begun to fall in. "You know," I said, "I think it's right up ahead somewhere." A few minutes later we topped a gentle rise and there, 50 yards ahead, was the biggest bull moose I ever saw or expect to see. He was enormous, with a fully-developed spread of antlers. A prize trophy if ever there was one. He had turned around and was facing us, standing in the middle of the road in a shallow depression, the whole scene framed in the red and gold foliage then at its height. Absolutely gorgeous. I would have given anything for a camera loaded with color film. At that, I would probably have been accused of photographing an unusually good piece of calendar-art: the sort of thing nature societies (and ammunition companies) publish. It was that good. The moose stared at us. We stared at the moose. Nobody moved for about five minutes. Then the moose turned and trotted into a densely-tangled blowdown just off the road. In turn we trotted down the road to where the moose had stood, expecting to watch it as it moved on down the depression toward the lake. But the moose was gone. For all his tremendous size, weight, and wide antlers, he had moved through that blow-down swiftly and silently, over ground covered with dead leaves. It was incredible. I don't think I would believe it if somebody told me such a story, but I saw it—and didn't hear it.

Other moose are not so adroit. There was Gertrude, for example. Why Gertrude? "Because she looked like someone who would be named Gertrude," said Bruce Andrews when he discovered her. She was standing in the iced-over swamp of Duck Cove, half way between solid ground and open ice, and she was in bad shape. She had apparently gone out onto the bare ice, slipped, and broken her pelvis in falling. Bruce herded her back to the woods once, but she soon returned to the same spot and would not, or could not, move again. For two days Bruce, Sherwood Copeland, and Warden Steve Hall tried to get Gertrude back on the mainland, to feed her, to help her in any way; all to no avail. As she became weaker, her hind legs splayed out more and more. Finally she developed pneumonia, and there was nothing to do but shoot her. So they did, and once more there was moose-meat around Onawa. But that time it didn't taste so good.

Clearly, a pathetic case. Classifying Alice Moore's moose story is not so easy, although it also contains elements of pathos. One day in the summer of 1979 Alice was plodding along the trail to her camp, and had reached the somewhat swampy area adjacent to Dead-man's Cove. Nearly bent double under the weight of her pack, Alice was simply putting one foot in front of the other along the well-worn trail when suddenly she was no longer looking at moss, rocks, leaves, twigs, and the usual trail-debris; she was looking at a pair of large hooves, with long, hairy legs attached to them. She looked up and directly into the face of a young moose.

She yelled. The moose grunted, stepped off the trail, and stood there regarding her with infinite sadness. Alice moved on nervously. The moose followed, bawling. "It was crying," said Alice, "I swear it was. That sounds nutty, but it was crying. It either thought I was its mother or wanted me to take it to her. It hung around camp all day, crying tears the size of golf balls."*

It may have been the same moose still looking for Mama that almost ran down Casey Bennett later that summer. There were four of us on a raspberry-hunting expedition around Flood Cove: Ayako and I, Marilyn and Casey. We had spread out a good deal, and as I was working my way up a gulley I didn't really know the whereabouts of anyone else except Casey, who had just topped the rise ahead and to the right of me where we had thought we could see an overgrown logging-road. So I was not too surprised when I caught a flicker of movement far to my left along the old road, at the edge of peripheral vision. But I was certainly surprised when it materialized as a large, four-footed, dark-colored something trotting through the waist-high grass and brambles. By the time I realized it was a moose it had gone up the hillside and disappeared beyond the spruce thicket where I had last seen Casey.

"Casey!" I yelled. "Look behind you!" And waited for the shot I was certain would follow. What I did hear was something else again: "Get out of here, you ugly sonofabitch!" A crashing of dead branches and underbrush, and a roar of laughter. Casey had not heard me, as a matter of fact, but he heard something charging down on him. He swung around, drawing his revolver as he did so, fully expecting to see a bear, which was the nominal reason for the revolver anyhow. No less astonished than Casey himself, the moose swerved off the road into a tangle of fallen trees, floundered around for several minutes, and extricated itself just as I finally arrived on the scene. We still refer to it as the hit-and-run (almost) moose.

---

*"As the size of tears is governed by the density and surface tension of the fluid, which is about the same for all animals, these giant tears seem to have been in the eye of the beholder."
—Comment by Dr. C. W. McCutchen, of The National Institutes of Health, Bethesda, MD, who kindly reviewed this manuscript. They may even have been in the author's omniscient eye.

MOSQUITOES ∗ Probably I first heard the story in the Yukon Territory, but it is no less true of Onawa mosquitoes: about the man who woke up in his camp one night and saw two enormous pairs of eyes staring at him from the foot of the bed. And he heard two voices:

— Shall we eat him here or take him home?

— Better here. At home the big ones will take him away from us.

* Ordinary wasps are a pain in the neck or wherever **MUD-DAUBER** they happen to get you, but mud-daubers are a royal **WASPS** pain in the . . . shutter-pin holes. Occasionally old-style keyholes, outside faucets, and anywhere else a small hole presents itself, but mainly the shutter-pin holes in the window and door frames of the big camp.

The winter storm shutters are not decorative items but rather functional protection against weather and vandalism alike. They are built of $3/4''$ boards with reinforcing crosspieces screwed top, bottom, and center, individually fitted to each window and door frame, and when in place a $2'' \times 1/4''$ iron bar is bolted across. But to lock them in position before the bar is added there are short cast-iron pins at the top and barrel-bolts on the bottom, two apiece, which must be fitted into matching holes in the frame. So the drill is to hold the shutter at a shallow angle relative to the frame while inserting the upper pins into their holes, then with the barrel-bolts retracted swing it into position for an exact, tight fit—which usually means kicking one corner because the window frames are mostly not square after nearly 100 years settling (despite a lot of jacking) while the shutters are. If Ayako is inside she then drops the barrel-bolts into their holes in the window-sill, closes the window and, after I have swung up the free end of the iron bar and pushed the $10''$ bolt through the wall, adds the nut. If she is not I must walk around the porch to the nearest door, go inside, and do it myself. Not a very tough routine, but with 19 such arrangements to make it can be annoying.

Nothing, however, even remotely like the annoyance of struggling to fit a shutter in place which will not go—and finding the reason to be that the mud-daubers have plugged one or more of the shutter-pin holes. It is that tight a fit, and there is nothing to do but clean out the cemented mud and cocoon with the narrow blade of my pocket knife. That is not too tough either, but the shutters are heavy and awkward—something like a small, stiff mattress—and one hoisting per window is quite enough. Mostly I check the holes beforehand, but sometimes I forget. Particularly when I am doing all this when the temperature is in the mid-30s with a matching 30 mph wind howling around the porch, catching the shutter like a sail and threatening to send us both either through the window or off into the pines—and then my language almost warms me.

✱ There is really little to say about muskrats; they are so much a part of normal life around the lake that no one pays any attention to them. A muskrat swimming across a cove excites no more comment than a loon, and their lodges in swampy areas are no more than a part of the scenery. They seem to feel pretty much the same way about man, neither seeking him out in the manner of chipmunks and chickadees, not fleeing with the alacrity of deer. It is a perfect case of peaceful coexistence. Except, of course, in trapping season. But that is something else entirely, and you have to be a year-round native with the constitution of an Eskimo to be involved.

Perhaps the only remarkable thing about muskrats is that there is virtually nothing remarkable about them. They eat a lot of mussels and leave the shells all over the shoreline and off the end of the dock. Their naked, rat-like tails are flattened in the vertical plane; a swimming muskrat uses his tail like a fish, but the visual effect is more like that of being closely followed by a snake. And there is nothing else worth comment. There are no stories, humorous or otherwise, about muskrats. The only thing that comes even close is the muskrat that lived in Bettison's cove some years ago; it must have been deformed in some way since it habitually held its tail straight up while swimming, which looked pretty silly. All it needed was a flag.

MUSSELS * Every few years someone around Onawa revives the old idea: if clams and oysters are such great delicacies, why not mussels? They are the same sort of thing, after all, and have the very considerable advantage of being free. Furthermore, you don't have to dig for them; any shallow cove will yield a bucket-full with little effort. So they are collected, and steamed or fried or whatever, and tasted—and usually thrown out. They are not particularly tough, nor are they really inedible, but there is a muddy taste that seems impossible to get rid of no matter how long they are soaked in clean water. Like most survival foods, they are certainly edible, but nothing you would want except for survival. Having read a good deal about such matters I once boiled a billycan full of rock-tripe or lichen just to see what it tasted like. The books were right; the result was a thick gelatinous soup that smelled rather nice and had no taste whatever. So I know I will never starve where rock-tripe and mussels are available, but neither do I gather them as eagerly as, say, strawberries, blueberries, raspberries, beechnuts, or pleurotis mushrooms.

On the other hand muskrats and raccoons could hardly survive without mussels, judging from the huge piles of shells littering the shoreline of any mussel-bed area. To support that kind of depredation mussels must have a very high reproduction rate. One would think they covered the bottom like pebbles on a shingle-beach, yet even in a well-musseled (ho-ho!) area they are usually separated from each other by several feet.

Finally, there is—or was—the world's slowest sport: mussel-racing. Nowadays little kids spend all day charging around the lake in boats powered by anything up to 25 HP motors, as soon as they are able to pull the starter-rope—sometimes by planting both feet on the transom. In the old days it required real strength (and far more importantly, experience and finesse in priming) to start a 10-horse K-35 Johnson, and besides that the thought of giving little kids complete freedom with boats simply did not occur. So we played kid-games, and one of these was to collect mussels, place them in a row in ankle-deep water, and see which would travel farthest and fastest. We quickly gave up checking progress every hour or so and the time limit was usually set for overnight. A slow mussel left a six-inch trail; a real racer plowed a three- or four-foot furrow. Zowie!

NUTHATCHES ✳ Nuthatches are nutty birds not only because they insist on coming down a tree trunk headfirst, unlike any sensible bird; they are also the world's most picky birds. A nuthatch at the sunflower-seed feeder will pick and throw out at least two dozen or more seeds before finding one it likes. Either that is carrying fastidiousness to extremes, or they have an agreement with the squirrels and chipmunks down on the porch. I suppose it should be considered a fine example of an accidentally symbiotic relationship, but on hearing that peculiar nasal "yank-yank" call I know that soon I will have to pack in another ten pounds of sunflower seeds.

* Ayako was once fishing at the inlet with a singular **OSPREY**
lack of success. No salmon, no trout, no chubs, no
nothing. She moved here and there; she changed bait;
she tried spinning with various lures; all to no avail.
She became annoyed; even the lovely scenery was a bit
irritating in its sameness when an osprey appeared far
overhead. Briefly, it scanned the area, then circled
lower and closer to her position. It folded wings,
dropped like a stone into the water some 30 yards away,
then flew off with what looked like a half-pound
salmon. Totally disgusted and convinced that the
osprey had taken the last fish in the whole upper end of
the lake—probably illegal at that—she gave up and
returned to camp.

But ospreys are not always so expert. I was once
sitting in the big boat on the east side of the dock,
working on the motor, with my back to the cove, when
there was a thunderous splash behind me: the sort of
thing that results from shot-putting a rock the size of a
loaf of bread as high and far as possible. Had anyone

else been around I would have thought it a scare-the-hell-out-of-him joke, but there wasn't, so I turned in amazement and saw an osprey struggling up out of the water in the middle of the cove. With empty claws. I knew they were big birds, small eagles, really, but never appreciated just how big until then. Also, I had never appreciated just how apt is Peterson's description of the osprey's call: "sounds annoyed." This one was certainly screaming in frustration. Beautiful—in all respects.

D. Bane

* Otters are wonderfully engaging animals, and it is **OTTERS**
unfortunate we do not see them more frequently
around Onawa. My own sightings are limited to half a
dozen or so, and it is likely that most of the summer
people have never seen one. On a number of occasions
when I have mentioned otters the response was an
incredulous, "You mean we have *otters* around
Onawa?" An otter-sighting is therefore something to be
talked about, particularly if is more than a quick
glimpse of one humping over the rocks and into the
woods, something like a racing version of a seal. The
thing is, of course, that otters prefer real peace and
quiet, rarely appearing until well after the Labor Day
exodus.

Some years ago Ayako and I had the good fortune
to watch a mother otter and her three pups as they
fished close to the dock. The mother would dive, surface with a minnow or chub in her mouth, chirp to the
pups who swam up to be fed, then dive again. It was
fascinating, as if they were deliberately putting on a
show for us. Certainly they were aware of our presence—Ayako was sitting on the dock while I was on the
boathouse porch—yet they seemed not in the least
concerned. It was completely different from the profes-
sionally-staged raccoon act: a simple demonstration of
swimming and diving, all done with style and dignity.

OWLS * Owls reverse the old golden rule for children: they are heard but not seen. On almost any calm night we can step out onto the west porch and hear them across the lake on the slopes of Borestone. A deep, resonant "Hoo, hoo, hoo-hoo, hoo, hoo, hoo" marks the great horned owl, while the barred owl lives up to its nickname of "eight-hooter" by repeating the "hoo-hoo" couplet four times in a slightly higher pitch. Or so the books would have it; never having seen an owl in the act of calling I can neither confirm nor deny the accuracy of these identifications.

For that matter, I have seen few owls at any time, except the day-flying hawk owl—and an unforgettable incident in Buffalo when, at the height of a wild snowstorm, a snowy owl spent an hour or more perched on a utility pole in back of Cornell Aeronautical Laboratory. But I do recall an encounter along the old trail from Bodfish Farm to the boat landing on Long Pond Stream. The trees along the trail are very tall and well-separated, so when Ayako and I spotted a great horned owl sitting far up in an old rock maple we had an excellent view as it moved from tree to tree, preceding us—not alarmed but simply keeping its distance. Aside from the size of the bird—they're big—the most impressive thing was the silent flight. A raven, a hawk, a duck, any other big bird would have produced a lot of flapping and wind-in-the-feathers sounds. Not that owl. Completely and absolutely silent. I knew about the special sound-deadening feathers that account for this characteristic, but it was still eerie.

Soundless flight is strange enough, but most disconcerting of all are those huge, piercing eyes. The only birds with forward-facing eyes (I believe), it is no wonder they are the symbol of the goddess Athena and wisdom. To be stared at by a great horned owl is an experience second only to being judged by an eagle, particularly when the head can be turned completely around to look over the back. It is an indescribable

feeling, really, but my sister came pretty close with her comment on the stuffed great horned owl placed on a bracket high and to the left of the big-camp fireplace. The bird perches on a tree limb in a natural pose, staring out over the room, and like the definition of a good portrait those great golden eyes seem to follow you to any point in the room. It has been there as long as anyone can remember—presumably from Dr. Sanden's time in the 1890s—and so we grew up with it. "When I was very small," said my sister, "I thought it was God."

PARTRIDGE * Pronounced, of course, "pa'tridge." And like the word "cahoots" this was also a source of some confusion to me when I first ran across references to square-notch gunsights as Patridge Sights. I had learned to shoot using much older guns with V-notch sights, and I could see no reason why the square-notch type was especially suited for shooting "patridge." It was a long time before I discovered that the sight is named after its developer, one Col. Patridge.

Perfectly camouflaged, wily and elusive as its first cousin the spruce grouse is dumb, unexpected as the woodcock; the partridge is the hunter's delight and despair. Beyond any other animal it has an uncanny ability simply to vanish even when you know exactly where it is. Ayako and I once flushed a partridge near the spring across Onawa from camp. It did not fly, but trotted off behind a boulder about the size of a bureau. Since the area is an open beech-tree stand on a gentle uphill slope, we had an unobstructed view of the surrounding terrain. Ayako moved to the left, I went to the right, and when we were in a position to look behind the boulder there was nothing there. Every other time I have lost partridge in similar circumstances I can find the escape route; trees, rocks, shrubbery—there is always a screened path that is chosen with unerring instinct. But not that time. I still don't understand it.

The only answer I can think of is that the bird was not immediately behind the rock as expected but some distance beyond, crouched, motionless, and invisible against the forest-floor debris. Partridge have a remarkable ability to sense when they have or have not been seen, and an undetected partridge will remain frozen until it is very nearly stepped on. In the spring of 1975, for example, one of the first jobs we had upon opening camp was to clear away the wreckage where one of the big pines had snapped and fallen across the little sleeping-cabin during a particularly violent windstorm the previous fall. It took us several days to limb the tree, cut it up, and drag it away down the path to the old garden. Ken Allen had made emergency repairs to the roof right after the event, but we spent a few more days improving on that (rebuilding was not begun until that fall) with much more than the usual coming and going along the paths of the area. Finally we began clearing up the smaller branches that were not really in the way, and when I lifted one from its position beside the intersection of the little camp and the old garden pathways I was astounded to find a hen partridge sitting on her nest full of eggs. The branch was not big—it covered an area perhaps the·size of a large pillow case—nor were the needles particularly thick, but it had fallen concave-side down and made a cozy little shelter for the nest. We had worked and walked within feet and inches for the better part of a week, but the hen knew she was unseen and never moved.

It could be argued that the maternal instinct was also involved in this incident, and there is no doubt about that. When first discovered the hen moved off the nest no more than a foot or two, fanned out her tail and stood there looking at us; I have a couple of color slides to prove it. Whether she would have flown at us or away from us upon a really threatening movement I don't know. I replaced the branch, the hen went back to her nest, and except for a daily inspection to see if she was still there—the only way to tell was to look for that beady eye through an opening in the pine needles—we left her alone. I wish we could have seen the chicks, but we had to leave for a week or more, and when we returned the nest was empty.

Even granting the different circumstances, there is a certain nerves-of-steel characteristic here that seems unique to partridge. It is a most effective tactic when the bird is actually hunted and the question of danger/no danger is clearly stated. I am embarrassed to think of the number of times we have stalked partridge with deliberate patience, carefully looking over each and every bush, rock, and tree along the last-known flight

path—and then heard the bird fly in the opposite direction from well behind us. We know this and we watch for it, and the partridge still manage to sit motionless until we are well past and it is safe to fly the other way. It is frustrating in the extreme. One of the few times we ever won this game was through hunting with three people; Roger Kittridge and I moved ahead through a dense pine thicket while Ayako trailed us as a sort of a rear guard. Sure enough; the bird made its move after Roger and I had bypassed it, and Ayako took it with a single head-shot.

Partridge hunting around Onawa is much like fishing; you must forget about the purpose and enjoy the method. There are plenty of trout and salmon in Onawa, but to catch two or three for a full day's fishing is very good indeed, and taking the limit is unheard-of. So it is with partridge hunting. There are plenty around but they are damnably hard to find. There are no particular areas where they may be expected. The usual rules for good cover, food, water, etc., simply do not apply in the deep forest. One place is just about as good as another, and the partridge seem to be distributed at random. The only hunting method that guarantees taking partridge, which is not really hunting, is to drive the local roads very early in the morning. In the course of routine supply runs to Monson or Guilford, Elmer Berg, Ken Allen, and Bruce Andrews— all successive owners of the Onawa General Store— shot far more partridge than hunters ever do.

Otherwise, the best thing to do is to pick a fine afternoon when the leaves are in full color, dress as lightly as possible according to the temperature, take an accurate, sling-equipped .22, a small rucksack for binoculars, camera, chocolate bars, etc., (and possibly partridge) and go for a walk along any of the old logging roads. Enjoy the red and gold and green leaves, the blue sky and white clouds, the chattering red squirrel, the inquisitive chipmunk, the trailing chickadees, the raucous bluejays. Look for fingerling brook trout in the streams and maybe play with the water channels a bit, clearing or damming as seems most fun. Examine the roadside debris: rusty chains, cables and unidentifiable bits and pieces of heavy equipment from long ago; plastic oil cans, food wrappers, and cups left more recently. Observe tire tracks, footprints, hoof- and paw-prints in the sandy and muddy stretches; who has been here and how long ago? Consider the contrast between all this wilderness and 40,000 feet above, where a vapor trail marks a flying cattle car heading for Paris at 600 mph, or a KC-135 and a B-52 are locked together in a refueling operation like nothing in the world so much as a pair of copulating dragonflies—

But don't expect partridge. About once in every ten such walks you will see one far up the road when rounding a bend, and that is when to begin a careful stalk. The other nine times, however, if you see any birds at all they are certain to fly from the brush at the immediate roadside an instant after you have passed. A shotgun is useless in those circumstances, and even with a clean shot in the second or two before the bird disappears into the bush, who wants to carry such a heavy weapon for several miles or more? Hence the .22 on a sling. A partridge jumped in this manner will fly no more than 20 yards or so. The trick is then to find and take it with a head shot to avoid spoiling all that lovely breast meat. If the first shot is missed, you might as well give up right there. The second flight will go deep and far into the woods, and even if the bird can be found it is now forewarned and will fly as soon as it knows it has been spotted.

PHEASANT ✳ Unlike western New York where it seemed as if we had to kick them out of the way, pheasant are extremely rare around Onawa. In 1978 Ayako and I were astonished to see a pheasant along the Monson road— the only one we had even heard of since the state released a flock in the Bodfish Valley some years back. They vanished instantly, taken by the foxes, bobcats, minks, hawks, and other predators of the area. Elmer Berg saw the only one that survived; it was walking along the Willimantic road, heading south.

D.Bane

* Big, spectacular in its black-and-white plumage topped by a fiery red crest: I have infrequently seen but often heard these solitary birds. The usual description of the sound is that it is "machine-gun like." Those machine guns I have heard had a far more sharp and vicious sound, but the comparison is as good as any. And the trees they have worked on certainly look as if they had been used for target practice. .50 calibre at that. While I have never seen a pileated woodpecker actually hammering away, I cannot imagine what else could cause such damage. The little hairy and downy woodpeckers are far too small.

PILEATED WOODPECKER

The pileated woodpecker is the only local animal I know of that has a legend attributed to it. It is said that they are the souls of departed woodsmen: the old-time lumberjacks, guides, wood hermits, and the like. Lloyd Kelley tells a fine story that he heard from Arthur Bessey, who swore it was true. Arthur and Frank Witham were in the woods one day, and they spotted not one but *three* pileated woodpeckers, all perched on a single branch. Frank looked at the birds and said, "Well, there they are: Henry and Charlie and Bert; and if I had a gun I'd shoot Bert, 'cause he beat me once."

I know nothing of Henry Lane and Charlie Hill, but I know that Frank Witham was quite a real estate operator because I have seen the long, long lists of his transactions in the Piscataquis County Deeds Registry, and so it must have been particularly galling to be bested at his own game by Bert Davis, who was something else entirely.

When Grandfather bought the camp in 1919, Bert came with it as a guide. I barely remember him as the crusty old man who fixed my broken toys and made bow and arrow sets for me—one of the arrows is still around, in fact. He had a white walrus mustache, and always wore heavy black workman's trousers, a white shirt, and a beat-up fedora hat. He must have been quite a character, for my father thought the world of him, and I wish I had had the wit to write down my father's many stories about Bert. He was so much a part of life at camp in those days that he died there in his room in the old boathouse, in 1935, at a particularly awkward time when Aunt Isabel was the only one in camp. For that matter, hardly anyone was around, and so Lindley Bettison remembers being pressed into service as one of the group that carried out Bert in a wicker-basket coffin—

And speaking of that sort of thing, it is well worth recording Frank Witham's last words to Arthur Bessey (this also from Lloyd Kelley). Frank was very ill and knew that he was dying, and near the end he said, "Well, Arthur, if I don't see you in the future I'll see you in the pasture."

Real characters, all of them, including the pileated woodpeckers.

PORCUPINES

* If chipmunks, small birds, and mice live in a much faster dimension of time, then porcupines certainly live in its antithesis. They move so slowly that it is a wonder they are not the common example of lethargy instead of the sloth. This extreme slowness is even a bit annoying, to me at least. And that is unusual in considering the characteristics of wild animals. Turtles move slowly, but it is obvious that they are trying hard. Frogs, toads, herons, and other creatures are motionless for long intervals, but when they do move the speed seems commensurate with the purpose. Porcupines, on the other hand, just don't seem to give a damn. It is this attitude plus the lack of any natural enemies other than the fisher (and there aren't many of them around) that results in so many flattened porcupines along the roads.

Otherwise they are not often seen. One of the few live porcupines I have seen in twenty years was a young one we discovered in 1979 while stream-fishing in the spring. It was clinging to the upper branches of a small spruce tree, and regarded us solemnly while we looked it over from a few feet away. Ayako was fascinated—she had never seen a live one before—and I had almost forgotten what they look like with all their insides properly on the inside. After some minutes of mutual inspection the porcupine finally began to clamber down with such painful slowness that I muttered something like, "For God's sake, if you're going somewhere get a move on," and went back to fishing. And I am considered a man of much greater than normal patience.

I don't remember seeing them around camp in the old days, but they certainly left evidence of being there. They chewed young pine trees, cabin foundation posts, porch-boards, and the corners of the ice-house indiscriminately, but what really turned them on was salt. All animals need salt, of course, but porcupines are salt junkies. Anything touched by a hot, sweaty human body was gourmet fare to the porcupines, and wood-handled tools, particularly the garden tools, had to be carefully put away. On the other hand—or the other end, if you will—there was and still is KAHOOTS, which is a gem of true Americana: a log cabin three-holer. To you it might be an out-house, a backhouse, a privy, a Chic Sale, or any number of other generic terms, but to me it is a KAHOOTS because it says so in six-inch birchbark letters over the door. Growing up with that as a normal part of summertime life, it was years and years before I learned that the phrase "to be in cahoots with" had a very different meaning. I still cannot think of it in any other way, really—Well, as can

The Onawa Bestiary

easily be imagined, once in a while the porcupines would get in and chew around the seats, which made them rather splintery and most uncomfortable.

The biggest problem, however, was always the back steps to the kitchen porch. There, on Sunday afternoons, we made ice cream in the grand manner. The old hand-crank churn was placed on the third step and we grand-children took turns cranking or standing on the gear case to hold the whole affair in position. When the cranking motion required both hands and was pretty stiff even so, the ice cream was about done. John Sullivan gave it a final, brief thrashing, and we had our preliminary prize: the thickly coated dasher. And Oh-dear-God what marvelous ice cream that was. I often wonder if it was really that good or just an exceptionally pleasant childhood memory. Certainly nostalgia is involved, but I also think it really was that good. I know the adults considered the recipe used by Mrs. Esterbrook (our cook at the time) to be the best they knew of, and I know the cream was fresh off the tops of the six or eight milk bottles we carried back from the station every day. Then, too, the ice cream was a bit salty since it was impossible to prevent some leakage from the rock salt and ice mixture surrounding the container. That same strong brine soaked the steps, of course, and the porcupines loved it every bit as much as we did the ice cream. The result was that the steps had to be replaced every other year or so. I doubt that John begrudged the work.

RACCOONS ✳ Raccoons are so cute that I find them rather annoying. It is hard to define the exact reasons for this, but it has something to do with a feeling of being used, that I am being forced to accept the sympathetic fallacy even while knowing perfectly well that it *is* a fallacy. From southern local-color coon hunting stories to Davy Crockett's coonskin cap to collegiate coonskin coats to the wonderful world of Disney and the ain't-nature-grand nature film, the raccoon is too much with us. It is the Bambi syndrome in spades.

So under the sheer weight of propaganda I am just as much affected as anyone else when that oh-so-cute masked face appears in the flashlight beam—but I don't care much for cleaning up the contents of the overturned garbage can. And it is all very amusing to discover that the coons have come down the chimney and made a nest on the shelf behind the fireplace damper—but clearing out the accumulated mess is not only distasteful but nearly asphyxiating as the hard-packed crap is broken up and scraped out. There are elements of true comedy in many other coon stories around Onawa, to be sure, and it was genuinely moving to watch old three-legged mama hold back while her babies were fed *hors d'oeuvres* when they all appeared at a Bettison north-porch cocktail party—but even as I watched I couldn't help feeling that it was so spectacular a "happening" that it was all carefully planned. It

had that unreal quality of a highly-organized sponta-
neous demonstration. Other favorite wild animals remain essentially wild, no matter how appealing; raccoons are professional actors, and there's the
difference.

The Onawa Bestiary   **97**

RAVENS * Ravens are very magical birds. They are prominent in Scandanavian mythology and Anglo-Saxon literature, they are one of the chief totem-animals of the American Indians, and I have no doubt that they are of similar importance in the folklore of northern Asia and any other regions they inhabit. One may dismiss this as mere primitive superstition, but it goes a lot deeper than that. Modern, enlightened, rational man thinks very little about a crow, if at all, yet automatically associates the raven with dark and mysterious ways and events. Edgar Allan Poe could not possibly have used any other symbolic animal as the subject of his justly famous poem. There is no living creature quite like it. The black cat is the only animal that comes even close, and that is still a long way off. The black cat is more of an omen or harbinger: the raven, on the other hand, seems to be a participant in events, if not actually causing them. There is intelligence behind the raven; it is significant that the god Odin's ravens were named *Huginn* and *Muninn*, thought and memory. So the ravens of the Tower of London are a lot more than mascots, and are treated accordingly. One of the Beefeater guards told me that, during the war, they got a better meat ration than he did.

I think I know why: because the raven talks. It is true that the usual raven-call is a hoarse croaking (quite unlike the cawing of a crow) and this is what is commonly heard. But the raven is also capable of an amazing variety of sounds that are remarkably like indistinct speech. On a still day at Onawa I sometimes

D. Bane

wonder who is coming through the woods and why
they are talking so loudly. I stop whatever I am doing
and listen attentively. The voices are clear but just
beyond the level of intelligibility—and then I realize I
am hearing a pair of ravens sitting in the tall pines out
on the back point.

During a visit to Terris Moore's camp on Borestone,
I took a canoe and went fly-fishing on Sunset Pond. As I
paddled slowly along the western shore a raven followed my progress atop the rockfall down the steep
slope of this crater-like pond. It paralleled my movement exactly, hopping and flapping from one boulder
to the next, and all the while talking to me. That it was
talking I had no doubt; the maddening thing was that
the language was familiar but not quite understandable. It was like listening to a conversation at the next
table in a sidewalk cafe; it was just a little too fast to
understand. I couldn't quite make out whether the
raven was telling me where to fish, commenting on my
paddling technique, or reporting the state of the world
as Odin's ravens were said to do. It was weird.

It was this incident that convinced me the raven is
my own totem-animal. I don't know how the Indians

decide such things—I presume by some sort of star position, seasonal astrology—but I know I have been classified. Ravens appear at too many odd moments in my life. As we drove north along the Alcan Highway to the Yukon Territory in 1967, for example, a raven flew ahead of and no more than 10 feet above the car for several miles. The subsequent six weeks were among the strangest, and and most enjoyable, I have ever lived. At Onawa, whenever the ravens are close around camp I know that something unusual will happen. Not necessarily good or bad, just unusual. Like any serious oracle, the ravens are enigmatic.

For all of that, the ravens have their lighter moments. Occasionally a flock of them—unusual in itself for otherwise solitary birds—can be seen soaring in the updraft on the northwest shoulder of Borestone. Soaring is not really the term, however; they wheel and twist, climb and dive, turn and counterturn. It is the stately dance of sailplanes, not the frenzied aerobatics of powered aircraft. That they are merely enjoying themselves seems obvious. Even the oracle at Delphi needed a day off once in a while.

D. Bane

✱ There are those who consider red squirrels with the **RED** same attitude usually reserved for mice, black flies, **SQUIRRELS** mosquitoes, and other unavoidable plagues. But while it is true that they are destructive, the comedy they afford more than compensates for the irritations. Some people actively hunt them, each year wiping out the red squirrel population within range of their camps. I prefer to go around with scraps of galvanized flashing, old screen, and shingles, blocking any possible entrance-holes under the eaves and such places. This means I still have to sweep up the piles of pine-cone seeds left all over the porches and steps, but as the price of admission for a continuous show of barely-controlled nervous frenzy it is well worth it.

At times when the difficulties of maintaining a camp built for 20 but now used by 2 are somewhat overwhelming, a red squirrel can brighten the day a good deal. Sometimes it is nothing more than coming across a dried mushroom left in a particularly silly place: the soap-dish of the outside sink, the middle of a porch table, neatly balanced on the porch railing, or wedged in a window corner. At other times the sight of a red squirrel in a state of hysterical indecision—turning back and forth, this way and that, bouncing up and down as if on springs, chattering continuously—seems an all-too-clear mirror of my own frustrations, and a direct message as to the uselessness of such behavior.

And perhaps the only time I ever saw a wild animal look truly surprised involved a red squirrel. I watched a pair of red squirrels chasing each other up, down, and around the big white pine near the path to the log cabin. The tree is some four feet through at the butt, perfectly straight, and clear of all branches up to at least 30 feet or more: a grand old patriarch of a white pine. So the red squirrels scrabbled around with unusual speed and vigor. I didn't know if they were two antagonistic males, or male and female, but the show went on for some minutes. Around and around, up and down, around and around, down and up. And up into the first branches. There they were momentarily hidden from view until one suddenly appeared in mid-air—not jumping, I was astonished to see, but falling! Straight at me. Spread-eagled, he (that was now obvious) seemed to float like a leaf, with mouth open and eyes even wider than usual if that is possible: a look of amazement and incredulity that such an insulting thing could happen to *him*! He landed on the spongy turf beside me and bounced about a foot. He was still for a few seconds, then shook his head and ran off around the corner of the log cabin.

There are so many morals and conclusions that could be drawn from this incident that I have never been able to decide which is most appropriate. If any. Just like a red squirrel.

ROBINS

✻ It is un-American, of course, but I dislike robins. In spite of the red breast they seem drab and colorless, and their song is the most boring and repetitious of any bird call I know of. And loud. I cannot recall ever being awakened—hangover or not—by all those robins stomping around on the lawn, according to the old joke, but I have been awakened many times by one or more robins yelling their fool heads off just outside my window. Particularly in the fall when they gather in flocks before flying south. At times there are so many of them on the lawn and along the pathways that it seems like a barnyard full of bantam chickens.

A few years ago there was a great hue and cry from bird-watchers, naturalists, environmentalists, and other such folk when the newspapers reported that in both Maine and New Brunswick robins were being poisoned, shot, and otherwise persecuted by blueberry growers. They were, it seemed, a real menace as they descended on the fields in untold thousands, and were accordingly treated as such. Horrors! It didn't bother me at all.

And I have always felt a certain sympathy for the soldiers✻ on guard duty at the Onawa trestle during WW II. Elmer Berg ran the Onawa General Store then, and he wondered why they were buying so many boxes of .22 shot-shells. This is really useless ammunition for anything other than snakes, mice, and the smallest of small game. When Elmer learned they were shooting robins and eating them with great relish, he refused to sell any more such ammunition. Elmer likes robins. I don't.

✻The sergeant went on to more distinguished service in later years: Senator Brook of Massachusetts.

The Onawa Bestiary   **103**

SALMON * The subject of this poem is the Atlantic salmon, and the setting is that of the New Brunswick salmon rivers my father so dearly loved to fish. But since the land-locked salmon common to Onawa is simply a smaller version of the Atlantic—every bit as fine a fighting fish and just as delicious—and the basic theme is identical when transferred to the lake setting, it seems appropriate. The style owes something to both Villon and Chaucer.

Ballade de Gros Saumon

Fait dans l'honneur de mon pere

Tell me now, in what far pool
Do the thirty-five pounders lay?
Or the seven-pound grilse that rise, as a rule,
To strike at the close of day?
The ones that take in the sun's last ray
With a roll and a swirl and a flashing leap
A dry White Wulff or a Silver Grey—
Where are they all? In what hidden deep?

Up from the sea, in shimmering schools
To the rivers they make their unchanging
    way;
But when? And where? Ask the village fool
For answer as good as an expert's. Say:
Is it there in the rapids that catapult spray?
By those tangled roots do they sleep?
This bank or that? Or the bridge? But nay—
Where are they all? In what hidden deep?

Last year was better, the weather was cool,
The water had cleared by the end of May.
And hungry they were, and stubborn as
    mules
They fought on the line; an hour of play
For the big one that rose to a Yellow Fay
In that shallow run. Is that where they keep?
Fanning the sand in the heat of day?
Where are they all? In what hidden deep?

    L'envoi

Prince, look not on this sorry display;
I hook only parr, until I could weep.
But tell me once, for now, for today,
Where are they all? In what hidden deep?

*Explicit le ballade de gros saumon de H. Sherrerd,
fils.*

SANDPIPERS   ✳ Sandpipers are the mechanical toys of the bird-world. At Onawa they do not follow the ebb and flow of the waves on knitting-needle legs, advancing as the wave retreats, retreating as the wave advances, because there are no waves that big on the only sizeable sand beach, but they do flutter on seeming-rigid wings from rock to rock along the shoreline and when they alight you can almost hear the gears whirring as they go through their habitual bobbing motion. Two of them can look absurdly like an Alphonse and Gaston routine. Spiders incorporate principles of stress analysis in their webs, beavers are wonderful civil engineers, the motion of water-striders is pure mathematics, and many other animals demonstrate the physical sciences in one way or another, but always indirectly. The sandpiper is the only example of a living mechanism. Watching one it is not hard to feel that if it turns a little more *this* way or *that* way, the key in the back will be revealed, slowly unwinding.

On the other hand, a flock of sandpipers put on one of the most graceful, and certainly the most eerie, displays of flying I ever saw at Onawa or anywhere else. In early September of 1984, Bill Massey and I were taking water-quality readings one afternoon at the Inlet deep-hole. I had made the transparency measurements with a Secci disc, noted the temperature, and was filling out the data form when Bill exclaimed, "Good God, look at that!" and even as I looked up there was a rustling of air, a rush of many wings, and a huge flock of sand-pipers—easily a thousand and more—shot by the boat no more than ten or fifteen feet away. As we watched they headed straight into the Sand Beach cove and disappeared against the background of the forest and Benson mountain. Then a sudden flash of white at the east end of the beach as they wheeled *en masse* exposing the pure white undersides, followed by an equally sudden disappearance as the brown upper surfaces blended once again with the forest. A flash at the west end—then the middle—the west again—the east. They were not landing. I started the motor and Bill and I went full speed for the cove, slowed to avoid startling the flock as we entered, and stopped in the middle. And for ten minutes and more watched spellbound as the flock raced from one end of the beach to the other, appearing and disappearing, flashing on and off not like a bank of moving lights, but with the ghostly silence and flickering intensity of an active aurora. Smokelike, diaphanous, endlessly changing its form from compact mass to wavering filament: a living arabesque modulating to a secret rhythm—

—Except when they made forays out into the cove. Several times they did so, and for a few seconds we were immersed in the cloud of birds: to each side, overhead, even beneath us in the calm-water reflection. And the sound was like seeing unknown colors, a new sense-dimension beyond the normal five: the wind of their wings, the pure energy of flight. Fascinated by flight I have always wondered what it would be like to be a bird, and in those moments I knew better than I ever did as a pilot.

Eventually, the flock found its way out of the blind alley and, as Bill and I followed, rounded the point of The Pines, sped downlake, and vanished in the general direction of Ship Pond Stream. What was it all about? The flock must have been migrating. It came out of the mouth of Long Pond Stream and, flying only a few feet above the water, could not see that the Sand Beach cove was a trap instead of Ship Pond Stream and the valley leading directly south to Sebec. It must have been a strange experience for the flock, suddenly finding its route blocked. But for us it was far beyond strange; it was a once-in-a-lifetime event that carried a touch of the supernatural—

SHELDRAKE ✱ Although they are also ducks, around Onawa a distinction is made between Sheldrake (American Mergansers) and "real ducks."

I once designed, built, and flew an all-balsa, free-flight hydro gas model at Onawa; I called it the Sheldrake because of the unusually slender but rugged construction and none-too-graceful appearance. In an article on this design, later published in *Jr. American Modeler*, I explained that the Sheldrake is "a scrawny, untidy-looking, fish-eating duck." There is no reason to change that description, because it is true. At least the females usually seen around Onawa. Where your normal puddle-duck is sleek and glossy and plump, mouth-watering just to contemplate as a potential dinner, the Sheldrake's needle-like bill, scraggly crest, and lean, streamlined body designed for fast underwater swimming present an impression of nothing but bone and muscle. Efficient but unappetizing.

My father always insisted that the edibility of a duck is directly proportional to the size and shape of its bill. Big and broad, like the Shoveller, Canvasback, Mallard, Black, and so on—delicious; they feed on plants and grain. But small and sharp, like the Sheldrake, means a tough, stringy fish-eater. I think he was right. I never heard of anybody eating a Sheldrake any more than a loon, and indeed the only reference to the subject in any way that I know of is the hoary story of cooking a Sheldrake (or loon, or coot) along with an axhead (or brick) and so on.

Nevertheless, Sheldrake are great fun to watch. When first hatched the dozen to sixteen or more ducklings are as lovable little balls of fluff as any other baby ducks, and their antics as they skitter in pursuit of water-striders, dragonflies, and anything else that moves are vastly amusing. A couple of low quacks from mother brings them into line instantly and they sail on around the point. When they are almost full-grown, the same group—now down to perhaps eight of the original mob—offers the closest thing in nature to fast-motion movie film. They will sail into the cove sedately enough, but if a school of minnows is present all hell breaks loose. It cannot be described as anything other than a Keystone Kops routine. They rocket along the surface and instantaneously disappear beneath; they surface like tiny Polaris missiles and charge off in another direction. If the sun is right you can see them streaking along underwater like so many little torpedoes. And everywhere the minnows are frantically trying to escape; underwater, jumping into the air, and sometimes skipping along the surface like flying fish. And all this frenzied activity proceeds at 64 frames per second, not the normal 32. It's pretty wild.

Sheldrake will do other odd things. For instance: one tends to think of them as never getting more than six inches off the water, even in full flight. They need about 100 yards to take off on a calm day, and fly so low their wingtips frequently slap water on the downstroke. Only when sweeping around an island or point and encountering a boat will they pull up in a chandelle maneuver, reverse direction or at least veer off, then drop to wave-top height again and speed away. They're fast. But for all of that they sometimes like to sit on the ridge pole of the boathouse, usually early in the morning. For a better view of fish in the cove?

Perhaps. Yet that would not explain their penchant for also sitting on top of the big-camp chimney. Thirty feet up and completely surrounded by much taller pine, birch, and maple, that is no fish-spotting lookout. The guide books say very little about their nesting habits, but I read somewhere that they will occasionally nest in a hollow tree, so while it is hard to see how a tall stone tower with a vertical hole in it could be mistaken for a dead tree, that seems the only explanation. And are they exploring or simply being clumsy when they fall in? Twice, in years when the camp was not properly cared for and the chimneys were not capped for the winter, we opened in the spring and found Sheldrake in the living room. One had died very messily all over the place. The other was alive and scared the wits out of us as we went in and heard something scrabbling around in the darkness. (All windows are shuttered and barred for the winter.) It bit me several times before I finally captured it under the desk, and when I did get hold of it all I could feel under the feathers was bone and muscle—even granting its normal lean build, how long had it been since it had eaten? As I tossed it into the lake it bit me again. The good Samaritan act gets no thanks in the wild kingdom.

* Shrews have a reputation for fearlessness second to none; only the wolverine comes close, in which case it is a good thing there are no wolverines around Onawa. Or are there? It is supposed to be much too far south for wolverines, but Elmer Berg once caught a glimpse of an animal that was certainly nothing common to the area, and does not fit any other description in the various guide books—

At all events, there are shrews, and it is hard to imagine how anything either bigger or smaller could be quite so aggressive. All other wild animals that I have come on unexpectedly will do one of two things: freeze, and wait to see what my next move will be, or take instant flight. Not the shrew. It turns to the attack, and out of respect for such a tiny package of vindictiveness I get out of the way.

Ayako was once cutting the lawn with the old power-mower used for this twice-a-year chore when a shrew popped up in the grass immediately ahead. Instinctively, Ayako swerved to the side, and just as instinctively and unhesitatingly the shrew attacked the mower—and got itself cut in half. That, as the saying goes, is *real* guts football.

Perhaps the most sage comment on shrews, however, was that of Sam Aertker. In the fall of 1966 Sam and his wife Yoshie spent a week with us. We hunted partridge, we explored the beaver dams and other points of interest, and we enjoyed the most beautiful Indian Summer within the memory of living man. Never has an Onawa visitor been luckier for weather. But mainly Sam went bear hunting by himself. He covered Barren Mountain like a rug, because all the signs and indications were there the once I went with him and and we hunted slowly up to the rockfall. He never got his bear, but came close when he found very fresh tracks in a gravel pit along the old logging-road to the notch. He took up position behind a boulder that overlooked both pit and road and waited, making rabbit-in-distress calls from time to time. The day was still; he heard something moving toward him through the underbrush and dead leaves before hesitating and then drifting away—and the only thing he saw was a shrew hurrying along the tracks. "I think it was after the bear," said Sam.

SIDE-HILL
BOWGER

✳ All I know is that it was supposed to live on the upper slopes of Borestone Mountain—oddly enough Barren, Benson, nor Greenwood Mountains were never mentioned—and the legs on one side of its body were shorter than those on the other. Obviously, the way to capture it was to get it turned around, then run downhill after it as it rolled, and rolled, and rolled. Whether it circulated around Borestone in a clockwise or counter-clockwise direction was never stated, nor was its function in the scheme of things, if any, ever explained. The same sort of description is sometimes applied to New Hampshire cows, but they do have some purpose in life. Maybe the side-hill bowger was supposed to guard the long-lost silver mine; however, the only man who knew anything about that was Uncle Rob, who was a poet and had a very fertile imagination.

* When I told my old friend Deboorne Piggot about this projected book, and the rather different style in which I was writing it, he laughed and said, "You mean you're going to say 'there's a *!!!*//@%#&*()*! skunk living under the porch?' " I assured him I was not using language like that, except maybe in relation to black flies. But what really startled me was that I had completely forgotten skunks. At the very outset I had listed probably 90% of all subject-entries, and had written some 60 pages or more when this conversation occurred. How could I forget something as obvious and even inescapable as a skunk?

Very simple: there must be skunks around Onawa, but they stay out of sight and smell. As far back as I can remember there have been no skunk incidents around camp. I recall a few skunk-and-dog encounters 'way back when my father used to keep either an Irish or English setter—sometimes both—but these, I am quite certain, took place in south Jersey, not at Onawa. Strange. So let us be thankful for small favors and question not the wisdom of the Almighty.

SMELT *   On the line a smelt
Is hardly felt,
But in the dish
Absolutely delish!

Signs of a changing ecology: until the last ten to fifteen years, smelt were plentiful in Onawa. They were even a nuisance, albeit a pleasant one. Still-fishing over the deep hole you would feel a brief tug on the line and naturally assume it was a bite. Hopes rose in anticipation of a good salmon or trout—and then nothing. Five minutes, ten minutes—nothing more. Did it take the bait? So you reeled in, and found a smelt hanging there like a strip of limp cloth. Hardly a fair substitute, but a whole hell of a lot better than a bare hook. You could never be too unhappy about a couple of hours of such fishing that produced nothing but a good mess of smelt. You miss the excitement of playing and landing real game fish—the smelt not only doesn't fight back, it doesn't even offer passive resistance; it surrenders instantly—but it makes an awfully good breakfast.

And now they are all gone, or very nearly so. I wonder why?

* There are garter snakes and grass (or green) snakes; **SNAKES** the former anything up to eighteen inches or more, the latter usually eight to ten inches. Both can swim very well and are considered beneficial, although this depends on your point of view. A garter snake has to make a living, but so does a frog, and so every time I come across a garter snake with a half-swallowed frog in its distended jaws, I think of all the mosquitoes and black flies that frog might have eaten had it lived. On the other hand, the garter snakes also help to control the mouse population, and so I leave them alone. I have no idea what the grass snakes eat; crickets and suchlike, probably. To me they are simply animated little lengths of emerald-green cord. Very ornamental.

SNOW BUNTINGS * Snow buntings are the ornithological equivalent of the Ice Princess or Snow Queen: beautiful but of doubtful desirability. Certainly they are lovely little birds—all white touched here and there with soft brown—and seem quite tame. We first encountered them in late October while partridge hunting along the Barren road. Three or four foraged on the road immediately ahead, allowing us to approach within ten feet or less before moving a bit. Since their normal range is in the far Arctic around Northern Ellesmere Island and Greenland, this tameness is not too surprising; they simply don't know what men are. But any man who knows what they are has good reason to regard their beauty with mixed emotions; they are a sure sign of a tough winter ahead. A whole flock of them drifting across a field like a swirl of giant snowflakes is more than a harbinger; it is a promise of the uncountable smaller flakes to follow.

SPARROWS

✻ It is unfortunate that the common perception of the sparrow is that of the house sparrow—perhaps the least attractive of small birds. Drab-colored to begin with and usually dirty from hopping about gutters, with an uninteresting chirrup for a call, the house sparrow seems only too representative of the cities and larger towns it inhabits. And as if that were not enough, it is not even a true sparrow, but rather a weaver-finch.

At Onawa we have the real thing, and in a switch on the ancient city-versus-country routine, it is the country cousins that are by far the more spectacular in both dress and song. The white-throated sparrow, for example, with its pearl-gray breast, pure white throat, yellow spot between eye and bill, off-white head stripes, and one of the loveliest of all bird songs. "Poor John Peabody, Peabody," and hence the alternate name, "Peabody Bird." Or the white-crowned sparrow, look-ing somewhat the same but with three prominent white head-stripes. Seen from the back, these stripes meet to form a perfect cross, and when so many other birds are assigned religious symbolism, it seems odd this striking feature has been ignored. On second thought, perhaps not: if the cross were displayed on the breast the bird would be on every church calendar and program—particularly now, as this is written, during Easter weekend. A rear view, however, is not all that inspiring or appropriate.

Sparrows are the standard literary epithet for al-most any small bird from the Bible to the present day, and it would be interesting to know how many of these references were inspired by real sparrows. What kind of bird did Matthew have in mind when he quoted Jesus to the effect that nothing escapes God's notice, not even the fall of a sparrow? King James' translators probably thought of the English sparrow or common house sparrow, which is not really a sparrow as noted above. Catullus immortalized Lesbia's "honeyed pet" in his *Elegy on Lesbia's Sparrow*, with its heartbreaking image of the bird on its way to the underworld:

> Now to that dreary bourne
> Whence none can e'er return
> Poor little sparrow wings his weary flight . . .
> (Translation by James Cranstoun)

But it is unlikely that an aristocratic Roman lady would have kept a grubby little house or city sparrow for a pet. A real songbird is more probable, and a bright-colored one at that. The Roman equivalent of a canary. On the other hand, Bede* probably *was* thinking of a sparrow in his account of the conversion to Christianity of King Eadwine of Northumbria in AD 625:

> . . . To his words another of the king's wise men and ealdormen gave assent, and took up the discussion and said thus: "In this fashion it seems to me, thou King, this present life of man on earth, in comparison with those times unknown to us, is such a thing as if you should be sitting at a feast amid thine ealdormen and thanes in wintertime, and the fire should illumine and warm thine hall, and it rains and storms and snows without; comes a sparrow and swiftly flies through that hall, coming in through one door, through another departing. Behold, in that time in which he is inside he is not touched by the storm of winter, but that is a single blink of an eye and the least space of time, for straightway he comes from winter and to that winter returns. So then this life of man appears for a little space of time; of what went before or what follows after we do not know. Therefore, if this new teaching brings anything certain and suitable, the worth of it is that we should follow it." In words similar to these the other ealdormen and the king's counsellors spoke.†

Bede wrote in Latin, about the year 731, and used the word *passer*; some 160 years later King Ælfred's translator rendered this into the Old English (or Anglo-

---

*"The Venomous Bead," to admirers of that classic of humorous history, *1066 And All That*.

†Translated from a textbook transcription of Old English MS 279 (11) Corpus Christi College, Oxford, (Ker 354); an early eleventh-century copy, perhaps several times removed, of King Ælfred's translation of Bede. If the text sounds a bit stilted it is because the word order of Old English is quite different. A re-writing in modern style would be smoother and tell the same story, but would lack the essential characteristics of Old English. King Ælfred and his translators thought and wrote in a different pattern, which is worth noting.

Saxon) *spearwa*; both translate directly as *sparrow*. Despite this positive language, a first reaction is that a swallow is the more likely candidate, since the first barn ever built undoubtedly had swallows swooping in and out the doors within ten minutes of completion. But the setting is winter, long after the swallows have flown south—which Bede, King Ælfred, and other so-called Dark Ages men knew quite well for all the other clangers dropped in the old bestiaries. Sparrows, however, are much more likely to winter over, and it is common (I have read somewhere) that they nest and roost in thatched roofs. Certainly they would have lived among the rafters and cross-beams of a great banqueting hall even as they now live in the steel truss-work of a suburban shopping mall. Some things don't change much.

On the shoreline about 20 feet east of the boat-house there is a roughly pyramid-shaped boulder that stands well above the surrounding scrub willow and bracken, perhaps ten feet high. The tip is a favorite singing spot each spring for a song sparrow, and it is therefore called "Sparrow Rock." Listening to him sing, it is nice to think that he is a direct link to King Ælfred's *spearwa*, Bede's *passer*, and King Eadwine's banqueting-hall of thirteen hundred years ago.

SPIDERS

✻ The way one feels about spiders depends entirely upon the circumstances of meeting them. There is instinctive revulsion when walking into the long anchor-strands of a web in seldom-used and probably dark places like the old laundry, the back of the toolshed, or the boathouse loft. The slightest touch on the face conjures visions of eight hairy legs, glittering eyes, mouth palps and fangs dripping venom, all moving with frightening speed along that strand straight to the face, the hair, down the collar—AAAAAARRRRRGH! But a few feet below on the boathouse porch the webs in the corners between the posts and roof plates are delicate works of art strung with dew-pearls on a foggy morning—

Or, in drier weather, hung with mosquitoes, flies (ordinary and black), small moths, and many other insects, some seemingly much too big to be so trapped. But spider-web is tough; remember the pressure of that strand across the face. Amazingly so. Until the advent of nylon monofilament it was one of the strongest materials known for its weight, and probably still is. The 1926 edition of the *Handbook of Chemistry and Physics*—a flea-market item that is nevertheless a good general-science reference work—notes that while single silk fibers may be used for reading-telescope cross hairs in an emergency, "spider web should be used in permanent work." Lest this be thought hopelessly obsolete and an example of how far science has since advanced, the 1975 *Columbia Encyclopedia* states that "Man uses spider silk for the crosshairs of certain optical instruments." The web is not only beautiful but useful.

Even so, spiders are generally disapproved of and classified with those other creatures of dark and evil ways: bats, snakes, rats, and the usual horror-story apparatus. It has a lot to do with living in unattractive places, of course, but there is also something about the method of using a web to make a living that seems offensive to the human experience. Face-to-face confrontation, slugging it out toe-to-toe; from swordsmen flailing away at each other to the high-noon fast-draw contest—that is the way to do it, not by patience and intelligence. It is all right and even heroic to kill and mutilate horribly with high explosives and jagged shell fragments, but gas is not fair. Not even a simple incapacitating gas that would result in a lot of prisoners and no wounded. Curious. The Roman gladiator with the

The Onawa Bestiary

net, the *retiarius*, is always the bad guy. Only commercial fishermen are allowed to use nets with no opprobrium.

Spiders sometimes make me wonder about the myths and legends of giants. Not so much as to the possible reality of an ancient race of giants (if there had been, bones and other archaeological evidence would have been found by now) but simply what it would be like to be confronted by such a being. A recognizable man five, ten or even a hundred times my own size? "A complete man," Ahab says, "after a desirable pattern."

> Imprimus, fifty feet high in his socks; then, chest modelled after the Thames Tunnel; then, legs with roots in 'em, to stay in one place; then, arms three feet through at the wrist; no heart at all, brass forehead, and about a quarter of an acre of fine brains; and let me see—shall I order eyes to see outward? No, but put a skylight on top of his head to illuminate inwards. There, take the order and away . . .

Aside from the philosophical aspects, there's a thought to give one pause. And what has this to do with spiders? Nothing, except that they show the greatest variation in size within a species that I can think of. At least around Onawa. A humming bird is tiny compared to a raven, let alone an eagle. A minnow is small compared to a 3-pound salmon. But the size ratio does not seem nearly as extreme as that between the big water spiders that hang around the dock and boats, and the almost-microscopic spiders that occasionally lower themselves on invisible filaments to hang in front of my book as I lie reading in bed at night. It is possible to think of amoeba, bacteria, and such true microscopic creatures as alive because we never see them; it is one of those scientific facts that one takes for granted. But a spider the size of a pinhead, complete with legs, eyes, heart, lungs, blood—all the mechanism of a functioning organism—alive and with a will of its own? Ridiculous. How would it feel if it ever ran into one of those monsters down on the dock? Probably about the same as I would when meeting Ahab's complete man.

SPRUCE
GROUSE * Only once have I ever seen spruce grouse around Onawa, or anywhere else for that matter. A covey of eight or ten were sitting in the lower branches of the young beech trees growing in the old logging-camp clearing at the head of Flood Cove. They took no alarm whatever as Ayako and I, and Lloyd Kelley with us, walked around and studied them from a few feet below. Indeed, they seemed as interested in us as we were in them. So it is easy to believe the hunting method described in Seton's *Rolf in the Woods*; a noose on the end of a pole is simply slipped over the neck and twisted tight. It is this ridiculous lack of fear—only of man, presumably, otherwise they wouldn't exist—that also accounts for the alternate name of "Fool Hens." They're all of that.

＊ Driving into Onawa one day in the spring of 1971, I **SUCKERS**
slowed the car for an habitual glance into the pools on
either side of the culvert where the stream from Little
Greenwood to Big Greenwood runs under the road—
and then came to a gravel-sliding halt. Both pools were
packed solid with fish, their dorsal fins waving just
above water like tiny shark-fins. Ayako went to the
downstream side, I went to the upstream side, and we
both stared in amazement. We had always hoped to see
a few brook trout or even small salmon, but this was
unbelievable. And no fishing equipment whatever.
Ayako was taking off her shoes and socks preparatory
to wading in when I remembered that we had something even better than normal fishing tackle: a new net
which we had just bought to replace those lost in the
boathouse fire.

She waded in anyway and began scooping up
whole netfulls of fish and dumping them at the roadside. Nice little six- to eight-inch fish, just right for
breakfast—and then I looked closer, and began to
laugh. They were suckers, of course, on the annual
spring run up the brook. Ayako had hardly heard of
such things and I had completely forgotten about it,
which was particularly embarrassing since my 1968
Downeast article on Great-grandfather Moore opened
with a story about exactly this sort of sucker-run in
Noisy Brook. So we threw them all back, went on in to
Onawa much chagrined, and have called that nameless
stream "Sucker Brook" ever since.

In Onawa, suckers can get pretty big. Worm-fishing

too close to the bottom practically guarantees catching one, and like everyone else I have been fooled many times into thinking I had something other than a one-pound plus sucker. At least until realizing it wasn't fighting hard enough to be a trout or salmon. It is too bad suckers are not considered good eating, and probably something that ought to be tested further. I admit I have never tried; considering the sucker's habit of vacuuming the bottom, it is not surprising they are said to taste rather muddy. But as is the case with many other trash fish it is also said that they are not all that bad if taken from very cold water in the winter or early spring. I think it was Joe Hartshorne who claimed sucker soup was quite acceptable. But then Joe also liked chub chowder (in cold weather, to be sure) was cross-eyed, a great story-teller, and one of the more memorable Onawa characters. So I don't know—

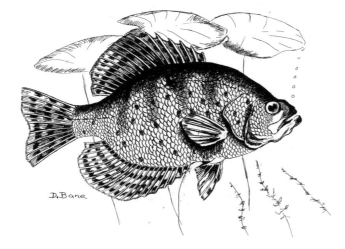

D.Bane

* Most fish are just fish: cold, silent, mindless crea- **SUNFISH**
tures living in an unseen world of water that is foreign
to the human experience. Even the gamest of game
fish, trout and salmon, do not impress me as anything
other than fish. Hence the expression that anyone
seemingly devoid of real humanity is "cold as a fish,"
and not in terms of temperature alone.

But sunfish are highly visible, preferring shallow,
warmwater coves where there are lots of interesting
places to live—near rocks, water plants, sunken logs
and tree trunks, and best of all under docks. The sunfish therefore assumes a definite personality, and a
somewhat pugnacious one at that. A sunfish hanging
in the water off the dock stares back at you with very
much an air of "OK, buddy, what do you want to make
of it?" And a whole group of them in a boat-shadow are
much like a gang of drugstore cowboys: nowhere to go,
nothing to do except make wisecracks about the passing minnows. If you take a bath in the lake, as opposed
to swimming, sunfish will nibble your legs as you
stand there soaping. Throw food of any sort to sunfish
and they will instantly snap it up, and just as likely spit
it out again. You can almost hear the "Ptooie!" As a
close relative of the bass, sunfish will fight as hard on
the line as anything their size and are good to eat,
although ordinarily too small to bother with. And a
sunfish guarding its clean-swept gravel nest will defend
it against far larger chubs or, presumably, anything
else.

A very tough little fish. With sides that feel like
coarse emery paper and a dorsal fin tipped with needles, the sunfish can afford to be self-confident.

SWALLOWS **✳** - What's he doing now?
- He's taking that motor apart.
- What's he doing that for?
- It doesn't run right, dummy.
- Don't you call me a dummy!
- Why not? You sit here every day and watch him do the same thing time after time.
- Hasn't he got anything else to do?
- Haven't you got anything better to do than ask fool questions?
- Don't you talk to me like that!
  (Exit twittering, out the front door.)

So say the swallows sitting on the boathouse cross beams, watching me as I work on motors, carpentry, or whatever. The most companionable of birds, in summertime I am never alone when working in the boathouse. Unlike chickadees, they cannot be tamed (and what would you feed them anyway? A handful of dead flies? Yech!) but they certainly like to be around man and apparently take great interest in his activities. They prefer sitting inside to outside, and while they will not sit directly over the workbench if I am there, yet they are always close—not off in another corner as might be expected. Their conversational twittering is constant, and it is impossible not to feel that they are discussing whatever I am doing at the moment. The occasional drawn-out rasping sound is uncomfortably derisory, particularly when I have just made a mistake. They are so much a part of the scene that I sometimes find myself talking to them, even stepping back to let them get a better view of the work and asking if they approve. And then I wonder if I really do spend too much time in the woods.

Such companionship has its drawbacks. The droppings here and there are not so bad, but when they attempt to build nests in the rafters the result is an awful mess of mud and straw that oversteps the limits even for a boathouse workshop. Inside nest-building is therefore passively discouraged. Whenever we return to Dexter we chase the swallows out of the loft before closing and locking up. After a few such incidents they abandon the idea of building inside and instead use the plate under the front-porch roof. They make the same mess there, naturally, but the rain washes it off every now and then and so it is no great matter.

One tends to think of wild creatures as having infallible instincts when it comes to raising young and

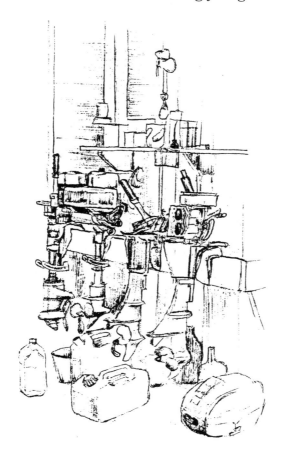

such real basics, but the swallows are a prime example that this is not necessarily so. Almost every year at least one pair nests on the plate as described—yet rarely do they raise a brood to maturity. Sometimes the nest is abandoned even before laying eggs; sometimes after the eggs are laid but never hatched. Most frequently however, and most sadly, the two or three chicks do not survive. They will be in all respects normal, healthy, and noisy for some days. Then they become noticeably quieter, and frequently fall out of the nest onto the porch. Wretched, scrawny little pinfeathered things; I pick them up and put them back—and an hour later they are on the porch again. The parents appear less and less, and the day finally comes when I look in the nest to find either a lone dead chick or nothing.

The only reason I can think of for this repeated ineptitude is that the nest becomes too hot. The plate whereon it rests is only a matter of two or three inches below the roofing boards, which are covered with tar paper and roll-roofing. The tar paper is black and the roll-roofing is very dark green; both colors ideally suited to absorb and re-radiate heat. I have never put a thermometer in the nest on a sunny day with no cooling breeze, but knowing how the whole boathouse will heat up under such conditions in the summer, it is most likely that the nest temperature must be well-nigh intolerable. And so the chicks must escape or roast alive.

Nevertheless, despite such depressing incidents the swallows are a joy to have around. Their acrobatic flying is justly legendary, and I can sit on the boathouse porch and watch them endlessly as they weave intricate patterns over the cove. If they left vapor trails then about 30-seconds worth would show as a series of marvelously graceful arabesques, but after that it would turn into something like a handful of snarled monofilament. And the best part of it is that they are consuming vast numbers of mosquitoes, black flies, and gnats all the time. Then too, it is always kind of interesting to walk in either boathouse door just as a swallow is leaving; it comes rocketing by my head in a dazzling display of maneuverability that is more than a bit disconcerting, particularly in early morning when I am not fully awake.

* Anyone who does not understand what Oliver **TOADS**
Cromwell meant when he said he wished to be painted
"warts and all" has never really looked at a toad. There
is no better definition of reality.

But thinking like that can get you into trouble.
Long ago when the whole family was in camp and all
the cabins were occupied, a lighted barn lantern was
hung from the ancient birch at the intersection of the
important pathways. So every night on the way to my
group's cabin I would note the big toad sitting motionless beneath the lantern, staring at it with what
seemed ineffable longing. It was there to catch the
cloud of 'nsects attracted by the light—I knew that
even as a small boy—but somehow that immovable
fascination bothered me. When I see a toad around
camp now and remember my thoughts of 40 and more
years ago, the symbolism of it all bothers me a good
deal more.

TREE-SQUEEK ✳ Unlike most fabulous creatures the tree-squeek has some basis in reality. The natural habitat is usually far up in the canopy of tall, skinny trees where everything is rather limber and tends to whip around in the wind with sufficient vigor to make the tree-squeek complain, at which time it may be located by the diligent observer. Occasionally, the tree-squeek will overcome its natural shyness and live at lower levels, closer to man and his works. (This is thought to be a degenerate mutational variety by some authorities.) These are mostly found in trees very close to buildings, and as a matter of fact there is one in the birch tree that has grown into contact with the eaves of the pumphouse. In a strong northwest wind it makes a pleasing counterpoint to the engine-and-pump machinery noises.

As far as I am aware, around Onawa only one specimen has ever been collected and displayed; it was taken by Bill Allen a few years ago and is nailed to his cabin wall on the front porch.

The Onawa Bestiary

TROUT The Maine State Museum in Augusta is an exceptional small museum, carefully planned and beautifully executed: a representative assembly of Maine artifacts and dioramas of the major environmental regions. The usual stock of dusty and uninteresting objects (eyeglasses and pen used by the Governor to sign the State Constitution, gown worn by his wife at the inaugural ball, etc.) in fly-specked glass cases so placed as to guarantee a blinding reflection from windows or overhead lights is happily absent. Everything is out there in the open, ready to use and obviously useful. The farm machinery would certainly run if required. The lumbering axes look razor-sharp and the big traction engine needs only fuel and oil to pull the whole building away. The fishing dory is seaworthy, the nets strong, and so on. No dilapidated relics here; only the real thing.

The trout in the "Mountains" diorama are real, too; shockingly so. Six or eight of them: big, fat, 2- to 3-pound brook trout, restlessly finning about a small pool in the granite boulders over which a stream descends. The other dioramas are extremely realistic—scenes of coastal life, marshland, inland waters, and woodlands are filled with flora and fauna typical of each, a 3-D photograph snapped at the instant of maximum interest, but necessarily frozen and lifeless no matter how ready to move the instant one looks away. The trout are something else, and without exception every visitor stops and stares at them in awe. "My God, they're alive!" is an expression often heard.

D. Bane

So they are, and it was a stroke of genius on the part of the designer to arrange things thus, for there is no better symbol of all that is clean and pure and unspoiled. Together with deer and wild ducks they are one of the great triad of wildlife symbols so beloved of the outdoors industry. Regular as the passing seasons and timed accordingly the magazine covers display them: the 8-point buck jumping a blowdown; the flock of wild ducks leaping from a dawn- or dusk-tinged marsh; and the trout rising to a dry fly. If animals could collect royalties all three species would have wealth beyond the dreams of avarice.

I read very little hunting, fishing, or other outdoor-sports literature, but doctor's and dentist's offices always have a plentiful supply of such magazines on hand, and in leafing through these it has seemed to me that articles on trout fishing approach the subject with a reverence not to be found in the other writings. Books on trout fishing are even more so, ranging from the lavishly-illustrated (and priced) coffee-table genre to privately-printed, beautifully-bound memoirs of retired generals, admirals, and corporation presidents, written with exquisitely literary style and consciousness. Trout fishing is different.

Indeed it is, and catching a trout in Onawa is always something special, something to be talked about when the salmon catch is merely noted in passing. There was the time we lucked into a mayfly hatch at the mouth of Ricker's Brook, when the trout were leaping about so wildly it seemed there were more in the air than in the water, and for 20 minutes or more I could not cast a fly without it being snapped up the instant it hit the water and sometimes before . . . And trout-fishing the streams is a delight in a class all by itself. Sitting in a boat trolling is pleasant enough in a mindless sort of way, but exploring along a mountain stream, slowly climbing from rock to rock, dropping a worm-baited hook or dry fly into the likely-looking pools here and there, is to be totally involved with life itself. The interaction of rock, water, moss, trees, shrubs, birds, sun, light, shadow, air, clouds, dead branches and live logs and saplings, mosquitoes and black flies, butterflies and water-striders—all is at once apparent, all is clear, all is harmony. It would be easy to become religious about it, and come to think of it, trout fishing is a kind of religion—*See? I'm doing it myself!*

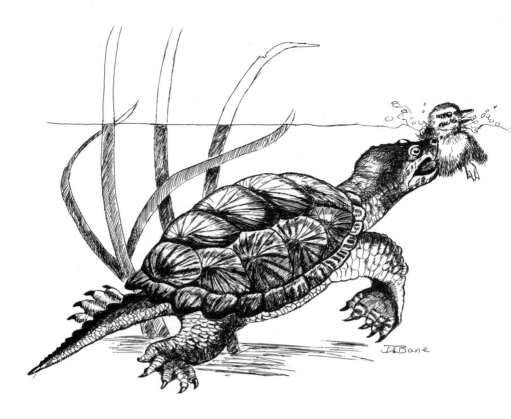

TURTLES ✳ Ken Allen once stopped by the camp to talk about
some work to be done or to have a drink, or both, and
then departed on down the lake. We had hardly walked
back to the big camp where I was repairing something
and Ayako was puttering around the kitchen, when we
heard Ken's boat returning. As we went down to the
boathouse again we could see Ken looking intently into
the bottom of his boat—he almost hit a couple of the
cove rocks for lack of attention to where he was going—
and poking at something with his paddle. Closer to the
dock he kicked at whatever it was and said, "Get back
there, you ugly sonofabitch!" Once landed he displayed
his prize: a huge snapping turtle he had almost run
down off Jay Donnan's dock. Did we have any interest
in or use for it, either as shell or meat?

Use, no, but interest, yes. We had occasionally seen
big snappers just under the surface, drifting along like
waiting submarines, and we once had a good look at
one sunning itself on a rock in the back cove, but
neither of us had ever seen a snapper at really close

range. There is little to report except that it bore no resemblance whatever to the clean, dry, inoffensive box-turtle or tortoise usually encountered. This was indeed an ugly sonofabitch, being big—about two feet from nose to tail—covered with slimy green crud, armed with formidable claws and beak, and having an extremely offensive smell. A singularly unattractive animal. Even had I known how to disassemble such a tank-like creature, for all the fame of snapper soup I would not have done it under any other than survival circumstances. So it was thrown back into the lake after a couple of photographs, and we all had another drink to celebrate the event and its immediate departure.

Probably we should have killed it if for no other reason than sheer ugliness. But there are other reasons, though of debatable validity. One is the danger of having fingers or toes snapped off; this is an example of those ancient cautionary tales that have never been know to actually happen. Probably because the days of transcendental nature-admiration with motionless fingers or toes trailing in the water are long gone, if indeed they ever existed. Still, it could happen—one look at that beak is very convincing. Another reason would be the taking of baby ducks. There is no more proof of this than the finger-and-toe business, but I can much more easily believe it. We rarely see snappers out in the middle of the lake; they stay close to shore in the same sheltered coves preferred by the Sheldrake families. A newly-hatched brood of baby Sheldrakes may number 12 to 16, but as the days and weeks go by this number is diminished by at least half with disheartening regularity. Baby ducks have many enemies, to be sure, yet I feel certain that many are lost as they inadvertently paddle over a waiting snapper. When we lived on the outskirts of Buffalo and fed a flock of several hundred halftame mallards that wintered on our backyard pond, I saw too many one-legged ducks to doubt this tale.

Certainly the snapper is to be treated with great respect. The *Encyclopedia Britannica* describes them as ". . . large, powerful creatures . . . notorious for their aggressive nature and the power of their jaws." Seton describes killing one and cutting its head off. With a rope tied to a hind leg and anchored to a tree, the body tried to return to the water for well over an hour. The jaws of the head convulsively clamped onto a thick branch and never let go. Another grim proof that reptiles are "very tenacious of life."

So while I am generally against killing just for the sake of proving you are a good shot, it didn't bother me at all when David Hager used his scoped .22-250 varmint rifle to blow the head off a big snapper that surfaced well out from the sand beach. No doubt the snapper has a place in the scheme of things—judging from the great number of diggings in any sand beach, no matter how small, the eggs are a favorite food for foxes and raccoons—but it's not hard to feel that we could really do without them.

* Or bog lemmings; it's hard to tell the difference **VOLES**
unless they can be compared, and although they are
probably around at all times only once were they really
obvious. That year they were not only obvious, they
qualified as a full-scale plague. They were everywhere:
running across the paths, under the porches and
cabins, climbing in the shrubbery and on tree stumps;
the lawn was so honeycombed with their tunnels
through the thick grass that you could hardly take a
step without a couple of voles popping out nearby and
skittering off to another tunnel entrance.

Since they were not getting inside and didn't seem
to be doing any great harm otherwise, we regarded all
this activity with a good deal of amusement. Then one
day Ayako went to pick some fresh vegetables in the
small garden she had planted in the old garden. It was
clear they had been at work, but there was little damage to the carrots, beets, or lettuce. When she went to
pick the string beans, however, half a dozen voles
leaped out of the foliage. Not only had they devoured
most of the young beans, but chewed the vines so
badly that in a few days they withered and died. We
didn't think think the voles were quite so amusing
after that, and were thankful when they returned to
their normal (unseen) population the next year. I like to
think that they were actually bog lemmings, and that,
like their Scandinavian relatives, they were suddenly
seized by an uncontrollable urge to swim across
Onawa—in the course of which migration they were
eaten by giant trout and salmon.

WARBLERS * "Jittery little birds," my sister calls them, and she is right about that; perhaps no other species is so constantly on the move, never still for an instant. One wonders if they are moving about even when asleep— or if they sleep at all. Flying jewelry, I call them, and consider that when God was finished with everything else He designed warblers just for the delight of doing so—and maybe as proof that perpetual motion is not impossible.

The only time I ever saw a warbler sit quietly was under highly unusual circumstances: on Monday, October 8, 1979, we left Onawa for Dexter with no plans to return until the weekend. Tuesday morning it began to snow lightly, then heavily up to 1 PM. With an accumulation of six inches or more, the temperature hovering in the low 30s, and not knowing what would come next, we made a quick trip to Onawa to drain the pipes just to be safe. It was strange to shovel all that snow out of the boat, and stranger still to see the birch and maple trees still in full color bowed—and sometimes broken—under the heavy, wet snow. Gorgeous. But strangest of all was the incident when we left. We were within a quarter of a mile of the south shore when I looked back up-lake and saw a small bird following us no more than ten feet astern, very low over the water, and obviously struggling to remain airborne. I cut power at once, the boat slowed, and the bird collapsed into the bow. A myrtle warbler. It perched on a seat for a minute or two, then hopped to the gunwale where it alternately eyed us and the distant shore. It took off

toward shore, fluttered about almost out of control, then returned to the gunwale where it sat quietly for the next few minutes as I slowly picked up speed again. When we were within a hundred yards of the shore it took off again and disappeared into the pines.

WATER-STRIDERS ✱ Water-striders are well-named, but they really ought to be called something like "the molecular bug" because they are the perfect illustration of at least two scientific phenomena dealing with molecules. First and most obvious is surface tension: that quality of water (or any liquid) whereby the surface layer of molecules acts like an extremely thin membrane which will support small objects actually denser than the liquid itself if they are not wetted—and upon which the striders skate about with such ease. It is, or used to be, a standard example of the phenomenon in elementary Physics textbooks. The second illustration is not standard, as far as I know, but it ought to be; the individual striders within a group move about purely at random, seemingly impelled by giant, invisible molecules of air in a dance of Brownian Motion. Brownian Motion is the irregular, zigzag movement of tiny (0.001 inch or less) particles suspended in still water. It is attributed to the thermal motion of the water molecules, and is a basic illustration of the kinetic theory of gases. Interestingly enough, although the phenomenon was first described by botanist Robert Brown in 1827, it was not satisfactorily explained until 1905—by Albert Einstein.

Most insects and animals appear to move at random, true, but there is something very precise and mathematical about the striders as they dart about in short, straight lines across the flat plane of calm water. It is an unnatural, mechanical sort of motion; one can almost see the grid of cartesian coordinates as the strider moves from X2Y3 to X5Y7 to X1Y4 to . . . And if you don't much care for mathematics there is something immensely satisfying about dropping a stone in the middle of a patch of striders, or slapping the water with a paddle, and seeing them all leap into the air and then go dashing around in even purer, more random, panic.

✳ There are not many people who know what a willi-pus-wallapus looks like, but I do. Because I have a picture of one. At least a picture of a carving, and that is just as good proof as reconstructing ice-age aurochs on the basis of neolithic bone-carvings and cave-paintings.

This carving was one of seven finials that topped the posts of the wide railing along the ramp in front of the old boathouse. There was an owl, a squirrel, a thunderbird, a trout, an eagle, a frog, and the willipus-wallapus. Except for the trout which was very expertly done by Uncle Bill Massey, all were carved by my father, who was not so expert but more enthusiastic. When he got tired of answering questions about this fearsome-looking creature, he added an inscription with its proper Latin name: "Willipus-Wallapus Ona-waensis." That seemed to satisfy everyone except little kids who wanted to know more about it, so my father would tell them the same thing he told me at that age: if I didn't watch out it would get me. He never specified just how it would "get me," and I still don't know. Probably just as well.

WILLIPUS-WALLAPUS

WOODCHUCKS   * I have known only three woodchucks around Onawa, and two of them recall pleasant memories of my father. The first and most directly concerned lived on our point, strangely enough, and must have strayed in from somewhere closer to civilization since it was not particularly disturbed by our presence. When we ate lunch and dinner on the north porch my father always threw some lettuce, carrot tops, salad remains, and the like over the side for Ginzburg (as he called it) who was generally waiting for this largesse. How a field-and-meadow animal ever got to the deep woods of our camp is hard to imagine, but there it was—at least during my two-week vacation at that time in the early 60s. It would seem to be a real accident, like the exotic European birds that occasionally show up along the coast and cause a sensation among bird-watchers, except that there was another chuck living under the big camp when we opened in the spring of 1980. We tried to feed it, but it was having none of that and vanished after a few days when it realized we were not just passing through.

The third chuck lived on the Bodfish Farm and was Sadie Drew's pet. In those days before the Onawa south-shore road we still came in the old, and hard, way through the valley. By this time the lower meadow was no longer useful for parking so cars were left at the farm itself, and this always meant passing the time of day with Sadie, Don, Mary, Chet, and whoever else was around. We had seen the pet chuck frequently, but on the occasion I particularly recall it was looking un-

usually fat and sleek as it waddled through the tall, thick, stand of weeds between the two old—Lord knows how old—cabins. Bodfish Farm was never what might be called a prime candidate for the unreal world of New England calendar art, yet even though the end was fast approaching this unattractive weed and bramble patch right in the middle of things seemed a bit much.

"For God's sake, Sadie," said my father, "why on earth don't you chop those awful-looking weeds there?"

Sadie looked at the peacefully browsing woodchuck and the chickens wandering about the edge of the weed patch. She looked at my father, then at the sky, and said slowly in her classic backwoods nasal twang:

"Well, Hen-ry, I keep it theah so's the chick-ens and the chuck hev a place to hide when the hawks is ovah-head."

WOODCOCK ✳ Every springtime, almost without fail, there is a woodcock living in the old garden, and equally without fail is my astonishment when it first explodes into flight at my feet. No other bird or animal that I know of (including partridge) remains concealed for so long—to the point of very nearly being stepped on—before fleeing. Even knowing that there is probably a woodcock around, it is always a moment of confusion.

And I am also confused about that flight. Everything I have ever read about woodcock hunting emphasizes the extremely erratic flight-path, and hence the difficulty of getting a hit. I see none of this; the area around the old garden is thickly wooded as is most of the old garden itself where we have not cleared it, yet the woodcock seems to follow a reasonably uncomplicated flightpath through it. Sometimes when carrying a .22 I have tracked a woodcock and thought that if I had a shotgun it would be an easy shot. But I never hunt them because there aren't any "them;" there is only one, and one woodcock would hardly be worth it for two of us—besides which I like having the bird around.

Many birds are credited with the old broken-wing trick. I am unsure about the others, but certainly the woodcock is an expert. I once jumped a woodcock near the shore facing Borestone and followed it as it stumbled and fluttered all the way across camp before realizing I was being had. I went back, hunted around very carefully, and eventually found a tiny ball of fluff with absurdly long beak and big eyes trying to hide under a dead leaf.

The End

About the Author

* *Henry D. M. Sherrerd, Jr. was born in 1928 in Haddonfield, N.J. He was educated at local Quaker schools and the Lawrenceville School, studied Aeronautical Engineering at Princeton University, English at Bowdoin College (B.A. cum laude 1956) and Mediaeval and Old English at the University of Maine Graduate School, where he won the Manfred A. Carter Poetry Prize in 1975 and again in 1976.*

In the intervals of this checkered academic career he has worked as an apprentice machinist, as a data analyst and strategic photo interpreter in the U.S.A.F. during the Korean War, as a technical editor-writer in aerospace research, and as a bartender in the Yukon Territory. In 1960, after a year of wandering around the world (literally) he married the former Ayako Ichikawa of Tokyo, Japan. Since moving to Dexter, Maine, in the early 1970s, he has been an outboard-motor mechanic, Assessor of Elliotsville Plantation, and map-maker.

His writings are equally varied. As an anonymous editor-writer he has written the equivalent of several books, and a number of technical film-scripts. His designs and articles on model aircraft have been published in modeling magazines. He has also written essays, articles, journals, poetry, and a full-length film-script for the Anglo-Saxon epic Beowulf. *There is something of all of this, and more, in* The Onawa Bestiary.

About the Artists

* *The realistic rendering of wildlife in* The Onawa Bestiary *is a specialty for Doug Bane, who has spent many hours in the woods observing animals in their natural surroundings.*

Doug, his wife Susanne, and their daughter Jessica live in an old farmhouse, which they are restoring, in Palmyra, Maine. In addition to painting, he also works at art restoration.

* *At the age of 25, Bill Massey has already been painting for more than half his life. Specializing in realistic oil portraits, he has had shows in Haddonfield, NJ (his home town), Philadelphia and New York City. He is a graduate of NYU (1985).*